KATALYA TREMAIN

This was more than an ordinary woman. What she might look like, or whether she was beautiful, was of no concern to Spock. It was her brain, her knowledge that thrilled him. To have the chance to learn her methods, to be beside her as she made her pronouncements on the intelligence of the Arachnians, that was Spock's desire. That decision could be a breakthrough comparable to the discovery of life in the sponge-rock colonies of Sentera V, or the lava worms of Phi-delta III. Knowledge was Spock's god, and Katalya Tremain was one of its prophets.

MUDD'S ANGELS adapted by J. A. Lawrence
PLANET OF JUDGMENT by Joe Haldeman
THE PRICE OF THE PHOENIX by Sondra Marshak
  and Myrna Culbreath
SPOCK, MESSIAH! A Star Trek Novel by Theodore R.
  Cogswell and Charles A. Spano, Jr.
SPOCK MUST DIE! by James Blish
STAR TREK 1 by James Blish
STAR TREK 2 by James Blish
STAR TREK 3 by James Blish
STAR TREK 4 by James Blish
STAR TREK 5 by James Blish
STAR TREK 6 by James Blish
STAR TREK 7 by James Blish
STAR TREK 8 by James Blish
STAR TREK 9 by James Blish
STAR TREK 10 by James Blish
STAR TREK 11 by James Blish
STAR TREK 12 by James Blish and J. A. Lawrence
STAR TREK: THE NEW VOYAGES edited by Sondra
  Marshak and Myrna Culbreath
STAR TREK: THE NEW VOYAGES 2 edited by Sondra
  Marshak and Myrna Culbreath
STAR TREK LIVES! by Jacqueline Lichtenberg,
  Sondra Marshak and Joan Winston
THE OFFICIAL STAR TREK COOKING MANUAL by
  Mary Ann Piccard
VULCAN! by Kathleen Sky

Star Trek Fotonovels™

1. CITY ON THE EDGE OF FOREVER
2. WHERE NO MAN HAS GONE BEFORE
3. THE TROUBLE WITH TRIBBLES
4. A TASTE OF ARMAGEDDON
5. METAMORPHOSIS
6. ALL OUR YESTERDAYS
7. THE GALILEO 7
8. A PIECE OF THE ACTION
9. DEVIL IN THE DARK
10. DAY OF THE DOVE
11. THE DEADLY YEARS

VULCAN!

Kathleen Sky

Introduction by David Gerrold

VULCAN
A Bantam Book / September 1978

ISBN 0–553–12137–5

Published simultaneously in the United States and Canada

Bantam Books are published by Bantam Books, Inc. Its trade-
mark, consisting of the words "Bantam Books" and the por-
trayal of a bantam, is registered in the United States Patent
Office and in other countries. Marca Registrada. Bantam
Books, Inc., 666 Fifth Avenue, New York, New York 10019.

PRINTED IN THE UNITED STATES OF AMERICA

This book is dedicated, with love,
to Dorothy Fontana,
who was there at the beginning. . . .

The authors would like to acknowledge the assistance of Dorothy Fontana in clarifying the facts about Vulcan sexual abilities, and her attempts to lay to rest the myth that Vulcans mate only once every seven years. . . .

Introduction

The cover on this book says that it was written by Kathleen Sky.

Don't you believe it.

It was written by Kathleen Sky, but it was extensively discussed with her husband Stephen Goldin —that is to say, Mr. Goldin participated in the creative process up to the point at which Ms. Sky sat down at the typewriter and put the words on the paper.

Some people think that this counts as a collaboration, but any writer will tell you that the *real* work happens at the typewriter in that narrow space between the keys and the paper.

Not that I am denigrating Stephen Goldin's contribution to this effort, you understand, but even Steve admits that this book is Kathleen's—and besides, he has a STAR TREK novel of his own in the works which will be hitting the newsstands shortly after this one. The point is that when you have two working writers in the same household, ideas tend to overlap, and it becomes very difficult to state that any book is purely the work of one writer or the other. Steve's STAR TREK book will have Kathleen's mindprints lavishly scattered throughout its pages.

There are those who will immediately suspect the most mercenary of reasons for my appearance in these pages—that I have been prevailed upon because my previous involvement with STAR TREK will somehow lend the cachet of significance to this work. (If you have been living in a cave since 1967 and do not recognize my name, I am the author of "The Trouble With Tribbles" episode of STAR TREK, as well as the author of *The World of Star Trek* and *The Trouble With Tribbles* nonfiction books, published by Ballantine Books; these three efforts, among others, seem to have established my credentials as a STAR TREK authority.)

Actually, the real reason why I am writing this introduction is because I insisted on it. I demanded the privilege of saying in print all the nice things about Steve and Kathleen that heretofore I have only been allowed to say in private or behind their backs, such being the perks of friendship.

Come with me now to those thrilling days of yesteryear. . . .

The first time I became aware that Kathleen Sky could write—I mean really *write*—was when I read her two-page description of Kaferah, the cat who loved cold oatmeal in spaghetti sauce. It was 1969, and she, Steve and myself were members of the Los Angeles Science Fantasy Society, a group known somewhat affectionately as "The Zoo." (In its forty-year history, the LASFS has boasted the membership of such luminaries as Robert A. Heinlein, Ray Bradbury, Ray Harryhausen, Harlan Ellison, Larry Niven, Jerry Pournelle and Alan Dean Foster.)

At that time, the LASFS had—it still does—an Amateur Press Association, which is kind of a mutual fanzine exchange. It works like this: each person publishes sixty or seventy copies of his fanzine—a two- or three-page effort—and brings the copies to the Thursday night meeting; all the zines are collated and each person receives a set of all the fanzines—it's called a "distribution" or a "disty" for short. Steve, Kathleen and I each had our own zine—there were some forty other contributors, too—my zine was entitled *Somewords,* Steve's was called #807691, and Kathleen's was *The Luminarian Wheel.* (Don't ask what these titles meant—even we didn't know; that's part of the rules of fanzine publishing. The publisher isn't allowed to know what his title means.)

Anyway, Kathleen's account of her misadventures with Kaferah brought a "yicch" to my throat.

It was only an anecdote, her discovery that Kaferah would eat anything if only Kathleen would put spaghetti sauce on it, but it was a perfect little gem of an anecdote; it was possibly the first time that Kathleen Sky was able to create an emotional reaction in her readers by the sheer power of her words alone. It was a beginning.

Remember, every great writer was a beginner once.

Kathleen was, in those prehistoric days, a *Trekkie*.

You see, in those days, when STAR TREK was still *alive*—not seventy-nine cans of syndicated reruns—there weren't many real STAR TREK fans; those of us who were felt as though we belonged to a secret society. Perhaps it seems hard to believe, but in 1969 there was no STAR TREK Phenomenon as we know it today, no STAR TREK books piled high on the bookracks, no STAR TREK conventions, no STAR TREK lunch boxes, posters, coloring books or fan clubs.

At that time, it seemed as if every Trekkie in the world wanted to write STAR TREK stories. As a budding professional at the time, I was sort of skeptical. The show had just been cancelled and there was no market anymore for STAR TREK stories. It seemed to me that if you were going to spend all that time at the typewriter working, you might as well write something of your own that you could sell and get paid for. Recent history has proven this attitude erroneous, of course, but at the time it very much seemed as though writing STAR TREK stories was a dead issue; but Kathleen—and thousands of other young men and women like her—wanted more STAR TREK, and if they had to, they'd write their own.

That's how most science fiction writers start: somewhere there's a young science fiction reader who can't find the book he wants to read, so he has to write it himself.

In those dark days, for a woman to write was "cute." The appropriate response was, "My my, isn't that interesting? Where do you find the time to write after you finish all your housework?" ("Housework?" Kathleen would respond. "Who does housework? You spend a whole day cleaning house and six months later you just have to do it all over again.") These kinds of comments were little more than verbal pats on the head. They were patronizing. Even people who should have known better didn't realize that women could write science fiction too.

Kathleen asked me for advice.

I told her that writing TREK stories was only a hobby. She should try to do something serious. Translation: something that someone would pay for.

It was almost a mistake.

I was putting together my first anthology at the time, a little thing called *Generation* for Dell Publishing. Kathleen began submitting her stories to me.

I do not remember most of her early efforts, but Kathleen is fond of telling one particular story about those first attempts. She claims she was a student of the David Gerrold Bludgeon and Blast school of science fiction criticism. Each week, with great temerity, she would hand me a new story. I—according to Kathleen—would read it, then throw all the pages up in the air and jump up and down on them as they fluttered helplessly to the ground, all the while yelling as loud as I could, "This is——, utter——!" She says I went through seven of her first writing efforts this way, and each time she got madder and madder at me for rejecting the stories. She would go off muttering, "I'll show that pompous——" And eventually she did. I bought her eighth story, a little nugget called "What the World Needs." I changed the title to "One Ordinary Day, With Box," which immediately started a whole new brouhaha, the outcome of which was that the title remained what I had changed it to, but a

whole new set of people were convinced that I was a
ruthless and uncaring troll who had trampled unfeel-
ingly across Kathleen's tender prose.

Kathleen is very fond of telling the above story.
I suppose it's true, if she says it is. She's a very honest
woman, and I've never known her to tell a lie, but I
don't remember any of it happening myself.

After a while, for some reason or other, I decided
to go off to Ireland—perhaps I wanted to practice my
drinking—and on an impulse, I asked Kathleen to
come with me. Instead, she married Stephen Goldin.
Well, first she moved in with him to see if it would
work. (Steve has never really thanked me properly,
by the way.) She didn't actually marry him until 1972,
and I was asked to be Best Person, which, I guess, was
their way of rubbing it in. Steve Goldin got Kathleen,
and I got to miss the Great Los Angeles Earthquake
and Exposition of 1971. (In fact, I didn't hear about
the latter until my landlady in Dublin passed me
on the stair one morning with a casual, "What didya
think o' the Earthquake, Davey-lad? The whole city of
Los Angeles was destroyed. Will you be wantin' some
tea?" The Irish are remarkably casual about disasters.)

Anyway, Kathleen kept pushing, always pushing.
She started selling more of her stories. Then she sold
her first novel, and then her second—and those of us
who knew and loved her recognized that she was beginning to reach her stride.

The nice thing about Kathleen's work is that it
keeps getting *better*.

Now, I will say a few words about Stephen Goldin.

Steve has been an imaginary companion most
of his life. It is only in the past few years that he has
become a real one. Recently, it has been discovered
that he leads a secret double-life as a were-koala.
Whenever there is a full moon, Steve sneaks out of the
house and climbs the nearest eucalyptus tree (there
is one in the front yard, but it has already been
stripped bare) and nibbles on its leaves. This can be

very embarrassing, especially when Kathleen has to go down to the animal shelter the following morning and claim him.

In most respects, Steve's history parallels Kathleen's, but at the risk of revealing great secrets I will tell a part of it that most acquaintances don't realize.

The average reader-fan-acquaintance tends to assume that science fiction writers are somehow "unique." There is the unspoken belief that we have more than casual experience with the things we write about, that the sense of authority in our descriptions of the workings of time-belts, artificial intelligences, spaceships and aliens comes from more than just our expertise in extrapolation and that, if the truth be known, we are actually all individual sources of great power and magic—we routinely hobnob with time-travelers and aliens. We talk to computers as equals and we travel by transporter and hyperdrive.

I wish it were true. It would simplify a lot of explanations. But the plain fact of the matter is that a lot of us who grow up to be science fiction writers start out as shy and frightened adolescents who are afraid of the responsibilities of impending adulthood. We retreat into escape and we burrow into a literature based on escape: science fiction and fantasy. We hide behind walls of make-believe so real that we don't have to make believe ourselves—and when we meet a kindred spirit, then there are two of us to help maintain the integrity of the walls that keep out the real world.

I was that kind of a kid. So was Steve. So was Kathleen.

But make-believe doesn't last forever. One day the sense of wonder starts to fatigue, the pixie dust dissolves in the sunlight and we start to see that the chinks are larger than the walls, and that our make-believe hasn't been very good.

At that point, there are two things a person can do. One is grow up. The other is to get better at make-believe.

Those of us who have become writers are the ones who chose the latter course. We looked at the holes in the walls, we knew they had to be repaired or reality would come creeping in. We learned how to repair them ourselves. Then we learned how to build new ones in our own images; then we built cities and peopled them with exciting heroes and fascinating heroines; we landscaped gardens, we erected towers and spires, we built ports and sent vast fleets of golden ships soaring into the skies. We conquered the oceans of night and spanned the galaxies with our imaginations.

And one day, we looked back and saw the walls we had once so carefully built. Those walls were not around us to protect us from reality—those walls were around reality to protect it from *us* and *our* visions. Reality is a fragile thing—it is a moment of *now* that continually collapses under the onslaught of the future; it is only a stepping stone called the present that exists uneasily between the once-was and the soon-to-be. Tomorrow's nows will be what we shape them to be— and this is why reality is so fragile and must be protected, because those of us who can make believe can see things that do not exist . . . and we have learned to bring them into being. Reality is at our mercy.

If it is a choice between growing up and getting better at making believe, I'll take the latter choice every time. That's what Steve and Kathleen have done —and they've done a better job of growing up than any ten people I know who have put their toys of make-believe aside.

In the past ten years, it has been my great privilege and joy to watch Steve and Kathleen learn and grow—not just as writers, but as human beings. In many ways, they have helped me and many of the other people around them to learn and grow as well. Theirs is a joyous home, filled with cats, books and good cooking—Kathleen makes a sauerbraten so mean that small children and animals are not allowed in the same room with it.

Right now, they are known in the science fiction community as competent professionals. I believe that they will both someday be landmarks in the genre. It won't happen immediately because neither Steve nor Kathleen is flashy; it will happen after they have built a body of work that is too solid to ignore.

Their best work is about to burst upon us and the science fiction pantheon will receive two powerful new gods. The potential has always been there to see, and in the years to come we will see it realized.

—which brings me to one final point. In the ten years that have passed, Kathleen has grown out of being a Trekkie, and grown into being a professional. Why, on the threshold of her success, is she finally doing a STAR TREK story now?

Why? Because the good people at Bantam asked her to write one.

You see, it's not enough to *want* to write STAR TREK stories, or any kind of stories, for that matter. You have to learn the disciplines involved; you have to want badly enough to do it that you will keep on pushing. If nothing else, this book is a testimony to that lesson.

Read. Enjoy. But do yourself a favor. When you're through reading, go back to the bookstore and hunt down some of Steve's and Kathleen's other books and enjoy those, too. Besides, someday they could be valuable collector's items.

DAVID GERROLD

February 1, 1978

1

Captain's Log, Stardate 6451.3:

Conditions in the Galactic magnetic field continue to deteriorate. Due to ion storms of unprecedented violence, the Neutral Zone separating the Federation from the Romulan Empire is shifting and will soon envelop the solar system containing the planet known as Arachnae, currently in Federation territory. Soon this system will be within Romulan space.

Our mission is to explore the system and search for intelligent life forms—and, if they exist, to aid them in avoiding Romulan domination. Star Fleet has assigned Dr. Katalya Tremain to the *Enterprise* to assist with the search for intelligent life. Though Dr. Tremain is the Federation's foremost expert on the exobiology of this region, I cannot help but worry about her. Commodore Stone's description of the woman as "difficult to work with" is entirely too cryptic for my peace of mind. . . .

Dr. Leonard McCoy had literally danced with excitement, and even Science Officer Spock had allowed himself the liberty of a slight smile when Captain James Kirk had told them that Dr. Tremain was being assigned to the *Enterprise*. The danger of the Romulans' proximity seemed to have completely vanished from the mind of either officer. They reminded

Kirk of overenergetic schoolboys who had been told they were going on an especially nice field trip with a well-loved teacher.

Kirk leaned back in his chair in the briefing room and watched the two men with some amusement. He hadn't seen the good doctor this happy since Scotty had learned how to synthesize Saurian brandy.

"Good grief, Jim, that woman's the best thing to happen to biology since Charles Darwin. If there's any intelligent life in that system, she'll find it! And a chance to work with her—it's unbelievable!" The doctor's blue eyes widened with awe. "She's won every award the Federation can give in that field, and a few they invented just for her! Why, I'm going to feel like a student again with her on board."

"I am forced to agree with the doctor," Spock said, trying hard not to grin. "Dr. Tremain's book on the *Diplopoda* of Marius IV is a landmark in its field. I, too, will be very glad of her presence on board, although it is unlikely that *I* will revert to student status. But then, there is a great deal I can learn from her; her mind more than equals my own—and, for a Terran, that's quite remarkable."

"All right, gentlemen, you've made your point. Dr. Tremain's arrival is a thing of beauty and a joy forever. We should be reaching Starbase Eleven in about three days. If the two of you are so much in agreement, Tremain must be one of the seven wonders of the Universe, and more than I can cope with. I'm giving both of you the job of acclimatizing her to the *Enterprise*. I'd hand it over to just one man, but Stone did say there'd be problems with her, and with the two of you taking charge, I won't have to deal with them. I'm going to be far too busy with this diplomacy thing Star Fleet's handed me; but I do warn you that the Commodore sounded less than enthusiastic about the lady."

"Now, Jim, important scientists like Tremain are entitled to their little quirks," McCoy said. "Even the best of us have problems in getting along with people."

The doctor glanced at Spock for a moment. "If I can get along with this Vulcan here, I should be able to get along with anyone."

Spock simply lifted one eyebrow and said nothing. The expression on his face was enough to convey his feelings.

"Besides," McCoy could not resist adding, "she's got to be more attractive than Spock, and more fun, too."

Kirk knew better than to enter into, or take sides in, one of McCoy's and Spock's mock battles once it got started. When his Chief Medical Officer and his Science Officer forgot the dignity of their respective positions and began acting like a pair of rambunctious siblings, it was generally a signal for him to leave. Spock, he could tell, was warming up for a comeback, and he would rather not be around to hear it.

"All right," he said over his shoulder as he walked out of the room, "I leave Dr. Tremain entirely to you. Try making her as comfortable as possible." Kirk was sure that his officers would take him at his word, and it might shortcircuit their feud for a while.

Kirk had problems enough of his own; and they, like the prospective presence of Dr. Tremain on his ship, were due to the shift in the Romulan Neutral Zone.

The Zone was a wide belt of magnetic field lines which marked the edges of Federation and Romulan territory. The magnetic flux of the Galaxy was a quantity that could be measured with great precision, and the field strengths were known to be constant over long periods of time. Since physical objects such as stars and planets were in leisurely motion around the galactic center, they could not be used as reliable guideposts for describing locations. Magnetic field strengths could be—and were—used in such a fashion.

When the peace treaty between the Federation and the Romulan Empire had been drafted, the Neutral Zone between them had been defined in terms of magnetic field strengths. Everyone had been positive the Galaxy's magnetic field would go on fulfilling its function for centuries—and so it would. The Zone would still be there—until the end of time, if necessary—but now its shape was changing, something its designers had never anticipated. Ion storms were sweeping across Romulan space, pushing at the Zone and forcing it to bulge dozens of parsecs outward. And in the path of that moving bulge was the Arachnae system. The *Enterprise* had been given the task of charting the bulge and, if possible, stopping it.

There was no way to stop it.

Each day it moved outward, changing the configuration of the Galaxy's magnetic field; and there was nothing that known science could do to change the fact that the Arachnae system—with its G-type star, seven planets, and possible intelligent life on Arachnae itself —would soon be a Romulan colony.

The Federation insisted that the Arachnians — if they were intelligent—had the right to their own form of government and the right to remain free, if such was their wish. This was not acceptable to the Romulans. The result: deadlock.

"Arachnae" might become another way of saying "war" if the *Enterprise*'s mission failed. But James Kirk had been told by the Federation Council that he could not fail—too much was at stake.

It had been argued that the Federation had no right to risk its own security for the freedom of an unknown race. But the vote had come down to one simple fact: if freedom was the ideal of the Federation, that freedom must be extended to any and all who wished it. The security of the Federation must not be placed above that belief. Without that central ideal, there was no Federation.

So Captain James Kirk had received orders to leave the advancing edges of the Neutral Zone and his studies of the moving ion storms, and report instead to Starbase Eleven to pick up Dr. Tremain.

Kirk had been given the honorary rank of Ambassador and the authority to treat with the people of Arachnae—and more important, to violate the Prime Directive if it became necessary in order to preserve the freedom of the Arachnians. That was a large responsibility, even for James Kirk.

Many of the Council members agreed with him. Ambassador Sarek of Vulcan, for one, was heard to remark that the cynicism of the Council was becoming a bit too bitter, even for him. He objected to the prevailing attitude of "like it or not, Prime Directive or not, *we* have the right to decide what is best for these people." Sarek felt that the Council was taking too much on itself in an attempt to play God with the Universe. Perhaps the Arachnians might even be better off or even profit from contact with the Romulans; could the Council deny that possibility?

The Council was not pleased with the Ambassador from Vulcan, and let him know in no uncertain terms that his comments were unacceptable in this situation.

Beings caught up in a holy cause rarely listen to rational voices.

The planet Arachnae had been dismissed as unimportant from the first day of its discovery—but let the Romulans have a chance at it, and suddenly Arachnae was the most valuable spot in the Galaxy. More important to Kirk, the Federation was sending *him* to straighten out *their* problem.

At first he had protested to Star Fleet that he was no diplomat, and that he was unskilled in this game. Why not send Gulied of Rigel, Meris of Andoria, or even Sarek himself? But Kirk was gently reminded of his own knowledge of the Romulan sector, based on the *Enterprise*'s patrols in that area. That made him an expert! The thought was laughable, even to Kirk. Simply by patrolling a sector of space that bordered the Neutral Zone, he became the only person in the United Federation of Planets capable of dealing with Arachnae. And he was supposed to be able to outguess and outmaneuver the Romulan High Command as well.

Kirk was beginning to have an almost paranoid itch that someone in the Council wanted the mission to fail. Sarek didn't believe in it, and there were those who agreed with him.

That itch became a certainty when he begged for expert help in establishing contact with the Arachnians, and had been told he was getting Dr. Katalya Tremain, a bona fide expert—but "difficult."

The ship was in orbit around Starbase Eleven. Kirk sat hunched in his command chair on the circular Bridge, watching the delicate maneuvers of Lieutenant Sulu as he brought the ship into a perfect elliptical orbit around the base. Kirk felt a brief stab of jealousy. The ship moved so quickly to do Sulu's bidding—but it was *his,* Kirk's, ship. The lieutenant, though, could do nothing without his Captain's permission—that much was true, and the thought was oddly comforting. Kirk sat back in his chair and asked for an estimated time of arrival over the assigned beam-up point.

"ETA six minutes, four seconds, Captain," Spock answered. The Vulcan's slender hands locked the coordinates into position. This was one beam-up that had to be perfect. Turning to face the Captain, he waited for the command to ready the Transporter Room and go to greet Dr. Tremain.

Kirk glanced at that impassive alien face and wondered what was happening behind it. Excitement, perhaps? He knew that Spock had spent the last few days reading everything in the computer library about Dr. Tremain, and had read and reread her many books on exobiology. Spock's mental preparation for the woman's actual presence on board ship had been carried out with incredible zeal, and his activities to ensure her comfort had been equally zealous. Her quarters were as pleasant as he could arrange them; he had laid in a stock of book-tapes he had thought she might enjoy; and had even, in a burst of very un-Spockian behavior, ordered the ship's hydroponics lab to provide some suitable plant life for the doctor's cabin.

Kirk smiled at the memory of Dr. McCoy's re-action to that last order. The doctor had made a similar request to the lab. His had been for armloads of roses; Spock had ordered her dwarf orange trees. When the good doctor kidded Spock about his choice of gifts for a lady, Spock had commented coldly that at least one could *eat* oranges!

McCoy had retaliated by providing a beautiful fur bed-throw and a bottle of rare brandy. Spock had then found a rotating model of a DNA mole-cule. It appeared as though the two officers might have made a game of escalating the luxuries they could provide Dr. Tremain, but Kirk was forced to call a halt when Spock caught McCoy taking over the Chem-istry Lab in an attempt to synthesize bubble bath.

The game was probably going to resume the min-ute the biologist was on board, and it was going to get very interesting for the crew—but it could also become a considerable problem, considering the tension that might arise over Arachnae. Kirk, too, had other wor-ries.

If she's pretty, we'll all be in trouble, he thought ruefully, knowing his own weakness for an attractive woman.

"Well, Spock, I guess you'd better get down to the Transporter Room before Bones starts to ingratiate himself too much with our expert. But do try to remain civil to McCoy in front of her. I don't want her get-ting the wrong opinion of the sort of ship I run."

"Civil?" Spock's eyebrows were threatening to vanish into his neatly combed bangs. "But Captain, I am *always* civil. It is impossible for a Vulcan to be otherwise. I assure you that I have no intention of be-ing less than a proper officer of Star Fleet in front of Dr. Tremain."

Kirk sighed. "Forgive my doubting you, Mr. Spock. Get down to the Transporter Room and welcome her aboard."

"That was my intention, sir." Spock strode to the door of the turbolift. "It is Dr. McCoy who should be reminded of his conduct as an officer—bubble bath! Really!"

The door closed before Spock could comment further.

Kirk shook his head in wonderment. *She had better be good,* he thought. *I never believed I would see the day Spock got this excited about anything, let alone a woman.*

But Kirk knew that this was more than an ordinary woman. What she might look like, or whether she was beautiful, was of no concern to Spock. It was her brain, her knowledge that thrilled him. To have the chance to learn her methods, to be beside her as she made her pronouncements on the intelligence of the Arachnians, that was Spock's desire. That decision could be a breakthrough comparable to the discovery of life in the sponge-rock colonies of Sentera V or the lava worms of Phi-delta III. Knowledge was Spock's god, and Katalya Tremain was one of its prophets.

Dr. McCoy was waiting in the Transporter Room. To Spock's consternation, he was wearing a formal dress uniform.

"I don't recall that being posted as uniform of the day, Doctor—and I am of the opinion that you have done this for the sole purpose of impressing Dr. Tremain. A rather childish gesture, even from you."

McCoy smoothed the silky fabric of his tunic. "I thought it would be a nice thing to do—show respect and all. Besides, it's flattering to my figure. I don't slouch the way you do, dress uniform or not."

"I do not slouch—my posture is merely relaxed."

Mr. Kyle's entry into the Transporter Room put an end to their discussion. Kyle took his place behind the transporter station and waited for the signal from the bridge that Dr. Tremain was ready to board the *Enterprise*. The signal came, and Kyle's hands pulled downward on the transporter levers. A shimmering column of light formed on the appropriate circle. Dr. Tremain was almost on board.

McCoy gave his tunic one final tug, and Spock, mindful of the doctor's comments about his posture, pulled himself rigidly to attention.

The shimmer of light coalesced into Katalya Tremain. She was very pretty. Not beautiful, but well proportioned. Her blue science officer's uniform fit perfectly over her small waist and hips and the curves of her full bosom. Her eyes were dark, warm as forest pools struck by sunlight; her hair a dark copper that complemented her tawny skin tones. Katalya wore the stripes of a full commander, but she looked as though she might be twenty, at most. Her appearance lied in her favor; she was thirty-five. Spock had looked up that fact while researching her history.

Dr. Tremain started to step out of the transporter chamber. She glanced around the room noticing Kyle and McCoy and then froze, staring at Spock. The expression on her face was unmistakable—hatred and loathing.

2

"I will not ship out with a Vulcan!" Dr. Tremain's voice was icy cold.

Spock stood rooted to the spot and said nothing. His face was a mask. It was as though he had not heard her comment.

Dr. McCoy, to fill an awkward gap, darted forward to grasp her hand and help her down from the platform. "I'm Leonard McCoy, and I want to welcome you to the *Enterprise*. I'm sure you'll find everything has been done for your comfort—" McCoy was babbling, but he felt that something must be done to overcome the chill in the room. He, too, was pretending he hadn't heard what she had said. Maybe the transporter was malfunctioning; perhaps Tremain was still dizzy and not fully focused.

"I want to speak to Commodore Stone, please," she said to Kyle, ignoring McCoy as thoroughly as she had ignored Spock. "There has been a mistake made, and I want to know who is responsible for this insult to me. And as soon as I speak to the Commodore, I insist on being beamed back down to the base."

Kyle stared at her, open-mouthed, unsure of what he should do. He glanced at Spock for some reassurance, but the Vulcan was as if carved from stone. McCoy moved toward the communications box on the wall and buzzed the Bridge.

"Captain, could you come down here a moment?

We're having a little difficulty." Getting an affirmative from the Bridge, McCoy then turned to Dr. Tremain to see what he could do to smooth over the situation. "Now, Doctor, Mr. Spock is our Science Officer, one of the best in the fleet, and he'll be working with you on the Arachnae project. Why, you couldn't get better help anywhere in the Galaxy. . . ."

"Did you hear what I said before, or are you deaf? I do not work with Vulcans." She stood with her arms crossed over her ample chest, tapping one foot impatiently on the tiled floor. "Are you going to contact Commodore Stone, Lieutenant," she said to Kyle, "or do I have to do it myself?"

"We'll wait till the Captain gets here," McCoy announced with some asperity. "He's the only one who can say whether you beam down or not." McCoy glanced at Spock to see what reaction the Vulcan might be having to the evident hatred from Tremain. Spock had relaxed and was seemingly oblivious to the fact that he was the principal cause of any problem. McCoy was tempted to suggest that the Vulcan leave until the matter was settled, but he had no right to issue such an order. The situation couldn't help but be an ordeal to the First Officer, McCoy reasoned; all thought of any rivalry or gamesplaying was completely swept out of McCoy's mind by Tremain's reaction. He wanted to say something to make things right for Spock, something to help that monumental pride he knew was part of the Vulcan's character. There was nothing he could do. There was no way to have Tremain's words unsaid.

The doors hissed open, and Kirk strode in, impatience written heavily on his handsome face. "This had better be important, gentlemen. I have a ship to get out of orbit, and I did give instructions that you two were to have complete charge of Dr. Tremain."

Kirk came to a halt in front of what he could see was a very lovely, very angry woman. "You must be Katalya Tremain." He smiled his best low-key seduction smile. "I hope there isn't anything wrong here—or anything that can't be quickly taken care of. . . ."

"Captain, I request to be returned to the base at once! A rather nasty practical joke has been played on me, and I don't find it amusing. I am sure Commodore Stone would never have assigned me to this ship. He knows my feelings about Vulcans. I will not work with this . . . this . . . thing!" She glared at Spock.

"Now wait a minute, Doctor!" Kirk grabbed her by one arm. "The first thing you learn about *my* ship is that I don't allow remarks of that nature; and second, yes, Commodore Stone *did* assign you to this ship. There's been no joke. You're here, and you'll stay here. That's an order."

"Please, Captain," she softened her tone immediately, "I beg you, let me contact Commodore Stone. There *has* been a mistake made." Tremain looked up at him with pleading in her eyes. Her abrupt switch in tactics had its desired effect. Kirk looked down at her, indecision taking the place of the anger he had so clearly felt.

"Spock," he called over his shoulder, "get up to the Bridge and prepare for leaving orbit. I'll take care of this problem."

"Please," Tremain covered his hand with her own. "Let me make the call."

"Captain," Spock interposed, "perhaps it would be best to *let* Dr. Tremain contact the Commodore. It should not take too long to establish the facts in this case."

"Fine. But I want you on the Bridge, Spock."

"I can deal with this, sir. There is no need to consider *my* feelings. I would find the Commodore's response interesting." Spock stood watching as Dr. Tremain's face darkened with anger. "I find this sort of bigotry fascinating—and I have *so* little opportunity to study it," he observed.

"Spock, to the Bridge; that's an order. It might not embarrass you, but it embarrasses the hell out of me." Kirk glanced back at his First Officer. "Please?" he added.

"Of course, sir." Spock turned smartly and walked stiff-backed out of the room. Tremain sighed with relief.

"Now, Dr. Tremain, let's get that call placed." Kirk signaled the Bridge, and a channel was opened to Commodore Stone's office. Stone obviously had been expecting the call.

"Let me speak to Katalya," the Commodore said, before Kirk could even tell him what was wrong. Once the doctor was in range of the screen, Stone smiled ruefully at her. "I'm sorry, love, but this had to be done. The orders came down from above. You're needed on Arachnae."

"But David—" Tremain's face, as well as her tone of voice, made it quite clear that she and Stone were more than slightly close friends. "You *know* how I feel about Vulcans; how could you have done this to me? There are other experts; how could you be so cruel?" From Stone's point of view, the tear forming in her eye was visible; neither Kirk nor McCoy could see her face that clearly from their vantage point.

"I didn't have any choice. And besides, I want you to get over that, and Spock can help. He's a good man, Katalya; trust me on that." Stone's voice was concerned; a real warmth for this woman filled his voice. "I can't keep on scheduling you on a basis of which ships have no Vulcans. You're making it too hard on me. I can't buck Star Fleet. This thing on Arachnae is too important for your feelings, or mine, to interfere. The Federation needs you at Arachnae, and the *Enterprise* is the ship in charge of that sector. Face it. There was nothing else I could do."

"Then I have to remain here." Even Kirk and McCoy could hear the pain in those words.

"Yes. I am sorry. Make the best of it. Kirk's a good captain. He'll manage things, I'm sure. Don't cross him; he's a bear when it comes to justice and tolerance on his ship. Try to learn something about Vulcans from Spock; that's the best advice I can offer you." Stone looked away for a moment, lost in thought, and then back at the screen. "Please don't blame this on me. Your happiness matters—it matters a lot—and you won't be happy until you get over this unreasonable attitude of yours. Have a good trip, my dear. Stone out." The screen went blank before Tremain could get out a protest. He was gone.

Kirk pushed past Tremain and signaled the Bridge. "Take us out of orbit, Mr. Spock. Dr. Tremain is staying on board. Commodore Stone's orders." Kirk waited for an acknowledgement from the First Officer, and then turned off the screen. He faced Dr. Tremain and said, "I want one thing made very clear. You will not insult my First Officer again. Do you understand? I don't care what your feelings are on the subject of Vulcans. While you're on board, you will treat him with the respect his position entitles him to; that is an order. Not just from me, but from Star Fleet. Now, Dr. McCoy is in charge of getting you settled in. I suggest you follow his advice on anything to do with the Medical section. Even though he carries the same rank as yourself, his position of Chief Medical Officer puts him one up. And if you're reluctant to deal with Spock, McCoy's word goes on the Science section, too. Any orders he gives regarding Science or Medical are to be obeyed. Do you understand?"

Dr. Tremain nodded. She had lost the battle, and seemed ready to accept that fact.

"Good." Kirk was pleased that the problem had been solved so easily. "Now maybe I can get back to the job of running this ship. Doctor, she's all yours." Kirk left the room quickly, the hiss of the door echoed by Dr. Tremain's sigh.

"I guess we'd better beam up my stuff," she said dispiritedly. "I seem to be here to stay."

"Begging your pardon, ma'am, but it's already up," Kyle said. "We beamed it up by freight transporter as soon as you came aboard."

"Stone seems to arrange things very thoroughly," Dr. Tremain remarked bitterly. "I wonder what he's up to. I thought he liked me. We were getting along so well. . . ."

"I think you're reading too much into this," McCoy said. "But it did sound as though you and the Commodore were still pretty snug. I got the impression that he thought this was for your own good. But I do wish he'd given some thought of what it might do to the *Enterprise*. The Captain and Spock are good friends, and Jim won't take kindly to any more remarks from you about Spock or Vulcans. He was, I think, considerate enough to allow you to handle the Science section through me. You have to admit that he is facing this problem halfway. The rest is up to you."

"All right, for the Captain's sake I won't say anything to his precious Vulcan—but I won't work with him!" Tremain moved closer to McCoy and smiled, trying to win his favor. "Try to understand my position. I was promised that I would never have to ship out with a Vulcan, *ever,* and now because of this Arachnae mess I'm having to put up with being around that long-eared devil. It's too much to expect of me."

"You'll get used to it. You have to. Come on, I'll show you to your quarters," McCoy said, mindful of Kyle listening avidly to every word Tremain said. In hours it would be all over the ship that the new woman on board hated Spock. McCoy couldn't blame Kyle much. The man respected the First Officer, and the fact of having a new bit of gossip to pass around would be too much of a temptation. One of the disadvantages of a ship like the *Enterprise* was that the same people saw each other day after day, and only had the same things to say to one another. Some new topic of conversation was as welcome as rain in the Sahara.

3

Being given the opportunity to acclimatize Dr. Tremain to the *Enterprise* by himself was a mixed blessing to Dr. McCoy. He was pleased that he wouldn't have to share her with Spock, but her attitude toward the Vulcan made him distinctly uneasy. It would have been quite different if she had, by personal choice, picked him over Spock—but it wasn't that simple. McCoy was, he knew, given to teasing the solemn Vulcan, but behind the jokes and pot-shots there was a genuine liking for the man. Spock had saved McCoy's life more times than he could count— and vice versa. Spock was not someone he could bring himself to like—not the way Jim Kirk liked him—but McCoy did respect Spock, and cared for the Vulcan more than he would rather admit. At the bottom line, Spock was one of the best Science Officers McCoy had every known. Tremain was forcing McCoy to examine his own feelings about Spock, and he wasn't enjoying the process. And it was complicated by the fact that, to McCoy, Katalya Tremain was a very desirable woman.

McCoy took Tremain to her quarters first, and she was more than pleased with them. She admired each of the changes that had been made in the standard visitor's section room, noted each improvement, and was loud in praise of what she supposed was his part in it. McCoy refrained from telling her just how much

16

Spock had done for the interior decorating. He quieted his conscience by thinking that she would probably have ordered them removed if she knew who had really provided them for her. He felt more at ease when the subject turned to the fur bedspread, and he told several tall tales about how he had acquired it. Katalya's appreciative laughter did a great deal toward stilling the small voice in the back of his mind which kept pointing out that this lovely woman was a bigot.

Tremain's luggage was standing in the middle of the room, and it seemed the most natural thing imaginable to offer to help her unpack. She readily agreed, saying that the job would go quicker that way, and they could get on to the regulation medical exam that much sooner.

They talked as they worked, and he found that they had the same tastes in books and art. She had brought some very good prints of two of his favorite Barrs, and an excellent Austin, which was one of the artist's more erotic pieces—but he liked it immensely. Much to his pleasure, he learned that Katalya Tremain was only a fair-to-middling chess player—very much like himself. She played guitar, and knew all his favorite songs. If it had not been for the ugly scene in the Transporter Room, McCoy could have felt himself completely at ease with the woman, and very attracted. In fact, a whole lot attracted.

As he unpacked a drawer full of soft, sheer nightrobes, McCoy felt that he had to know more about her phobia. The transparent garments, scented with lavender, were telling him a great deal about her romantic nature, and he wanted to know what sort of mental mine field he might have to walk through on the way to seeing her model those delicious bits of silk and lace. Spock and Vulcans were no competition for a pretty woman, nightgowns, and a bedroom.

"Tell me, Katalya," he said, tucking the last of the negligees away, "just why do you hate Vulcans so much? It's a sad flaw in a lady as nice as you are. It's a downright pity, too."

"I'd rather not talk about it, Len. It's not a subject I enjoy, and I'm still seething about the necessity of my being anywhere around the *Enterprise* and its Vulcan." Tremain placed the last of her uniforms in the closet and, dusting off her hands, turned to face McCoy. "There. All done. You were a terrific help, and I do appreciate it. Now, let's get my medical exam over, and then I want to see your labs."

"You're avoiding the subject, and changing it in that clumsy a fashion won't keep me from asking again what you have against Vulcans. You know quite well that a psychiatric exam is part of the physical. I'll be able to figure out a lot from that, and I can probably guess the rest. Why don't you make my job easier and just tell me what the problem is? I take it it's not Spock himself but all Vulcans who set you off."

Tremain sighed and covered her eyes with one hand for a moment. "I can't get close enough to the core of my feelings to be able to discuss it without falling apart. I've had more psych tests than I care to think about, and they only tell me one thing: I hate Vulcans. They're cold, underhanded, and treacherous. You can't trust them, no matter how much you think you know them. Logic, their own brand of logic, is the only thing that matters to them. That kind of disgusting ingratitude is more than I can stomach."

"You've had dealings with them in the past, I take it. Something to base your feelings on. Hate like yours should have some sort of reason, you know."

"It has a reason—a million reasons. I've shipped with Vulcans before, but I vowed I'd never do it again. And David Stone, and Star Fleet, have made me break my vow—is that enough for you, Doctor? You know, your prying is nothing new to me. There've been other men who tried to play doctor with my head." She sat down suddenly as though the effort of talking about her feelings was too much for her.

McCoy joined her on the fur-covered bed. He reached his arm around her unprotesting shoulder and pulled her closer. "I generally like to see what makes a lady tick before I start wanting to play doctor with her mind or body—and I mean that in the nonmedical sense."

McCoy grinned at her, waiting to see what she might say to his rather bald proposition. She was new to the ship, and he knew that as soon as the rest of the crew got a look at her, the offers would be coming thick and fast. It was better to be a little too hasty about this sort of thing than to run the risk of some fellow officer grabbing her up from under his eyes. He did hope she had no major hangups in the sexual area; it would be a waste of very good material if she did.

"What? You're going to forgive me for being prejudiced against Vulcans so quickly?" She tilted her head to look up at him. "You must have a very flexible mind, Doctor."

"No, just a well-compartmented one. I don't like the way you act about Vulcans, but I don't see anything about you as a woman to object to—or is there something I don't know?"

"I am sort of bespoke for. Commodore Stone and I have gotten close since I was assigned to his Starbase." She was smiling, and McCoy got the message that Stone did mean more than a little to her.

"Are you twoing?" he asked, expecting the answer almost before he'd finished the question. An engaged woman didn't usually carry a suitcase of sexy underthings with her on a trip if she wasn't intending to wear them for someone—and Stone was safely ensconced back on Starbase Eleven.

"Sort of—but we're not getting papers or anything. He's very married to his job, and in a way so am I. There's not even a term marriage coming up soon, if that's what you mean. He's been very good to me, and I am fond of him—but after this assignment, I might change my mind."

"But do you love him?" McCoy persisted. He could see some hope for himself in her last remark.

"Love." A shadow crossed her face. "No, not love. But I did care a great deal for him. David's helped pull me out of some pretty rotten moods, and I am grateful for that. Marriages have been formed on less, you know. And if we ever did marry, it'd probably only be for a single term. I don't want children."

"I've never liked the idea of term marriages. They're so cold," McCoy said. "Of course, my wife wanted a term marriage too when we got married, but I talked her out of it. I wanted the stability of a life partnership arrangement."

"Ah. So you *are* married. I take it you and your wife have some sort of agreement about your dalliance aboard ship. Or did I misinterpret your remarks to me a minute ago?" She was grinning like a cat at a mousehole, and McCoy knew full well she had caught him in an inconsistency and was enjoying every bit of it.

"I'm divorced," he said reluctantly. "My wife and I stayed together until after the birth of our child, Joanna. But we did love each other once, maybe even a lot, before we were married—and it was for more than the sake of a child."

"But it wasn't for life; and whether you intended it or not, it turned out to be a term marriage."

McCoy nodded and tried to think of a good answer for this comment. "The ending was nothing unusual . . . the thing just slowly fell apart. Different interests got in the way; I spent too much time on my work—and I had always wanted to go into space medicine. She didn't like that idea too much, so she talked me out of it." McCoy stopped speaking; his thoughts gradually coalesced into a pattern of regrets, blame and fault-finding. "I guess I resented that—more than I realized. I took it out on her by overwork, and not being home much. . . ."

"So she found someone else."

McCoy looked at Tremain, his eyes widening. "How did you know that?" he demanded. "Who've you been talking to on Starbase Eleven?"

"No one. I did the same thing with my marriage. He wanted to ship out, and even though I didn't want to, I shipped out with him. But I met someone else and things , , drifted. I think that's the best word for it."

"So you're divorced too. Welcome to the club. I can understand why you want a term marriage with Stone, but not all marriages are the same."

"Not divorced. Widowed. He didn't come back from that last trip out." She leaned her head against his shoulder. "I just didn't want to go into space one more time. And he did—and here I am. He's dead, and it's all too late. But then, it was too late even before he died."

"Was he a Vulcan?" McCoy asked, suspecting a possible explanation for her hatred.

The result was electric. She leaped off the bed and faced him, arms akimbo. "Don't you ever *dare* insinuate that I could ever touch a Vulcan, let alone —Damn you! It's the most disgusting thing you could ever say to me!" She was trembling with fury. McCoy moved toward her, trying to take her in his arms.

"Now stop that. I didn't mean—I only thought— that is—I've made a mess of it, haven't I? Please forgive me."

She relaxed slowly, and let him hold her. He could feel her body shaking against his, and there was a sniffling sound that made him positive she was crying.

"Do you have a handkerchief?" he said, patting her gently on the back. "Nearly every woman I know finds that she's lacking something to blow her nose on at times like this. I think it's because you all hate to admit you make a mess when you cry."

Dr. Tremain giggled soggily into his uniform. "You're right. We all think tears are such a great weapon that you big strong men should melt at the sight of them, and we forget about the messy parts like runny noses."

"That's my girl. Much better. Try to laugh now." McCoy fished a clean handkerchief out of a sleeve and gently wiped her wet face. "Now. Let's get your eyes a bit less red, and I'll take you down to the Medical section for your exam. Put some cold water

on your face. I'd hate to have my staff think I made
you cry; it would ruin my reputation as a demon
lover."

Tremain laughed and moved out of his arms. "I
think I like you, Leonard. I think I like you a lot. I'm
going to need someone like you just to get me through
this trip with my sanity intact. If only I could make
you understand how horrible it is to me to have that
Vulcan on board." She smiled up at him, a wet, watery
sort of smile. "I'll do my best on this assignment, but
I'll need your help. Will you give it to me? That is,
without forcing me to give up my basic feelings about
Vulcans? What I'm asking of you is that you try to
understand them. I don't want to change, you know."

McCoy fought down several conflicting emotions.
He wanted to cure her of her prejudice, keep her out
of trouble, and keep her for himself. He wasn't sure
how he could manage all of them at once, but he was
willing to break a blood vessel trying.

"Ah'll do any little thing Ah can for you, Katalya
honey," he said in his very best Southern accent. And
he meant it.

4

I am logging an official protest on having to carry Commander Katalya Tremain aboard my ship. Her manner and attitude toward my First Officer is a disgrace to her uniform and to Star Fleet. I will demand disciplinary action if there are any, repeat, any more scenes such as she enacted upon boarding the *Enterprise*. But what will happen when we get to Arachnae? Does she understand that she must work with Spock on the planet's surface? Why were we sent a woman guaranteed to be a problem, when we are in the middle of so delicate a situation?

James Kirk found himself troubled by feelings of rampant paranoia. He knew full well that there were delegates to the Federation Council who had been less than happy about risking so much over a race that might not even be sentient. Had one of those members insisted that Dr. Tremain be sent along for the sole purpose of destroying the Federation effort? Or, more paranoid still, could she be in the pay of the Romulans, and her great attack of hysteria over Spock merely a feint meant to throw them all off guard?

But Commodore Stone was a man so loyal to the Federation that any idea of his compliance with such a plot was laughable. He had sent Dr. Tremain to the *Enterprise* without warning her of Spock's presence,

23

and his warning to Kirk had been deliberately vague.
But that was not enough to pin an absolute suspicion
on. Kirk considered getting in touch with Stone and
demanding an explanation of his actions, but that was
a dangerous thing to do; almost an accusation of trea-
son, which would not sit well with the Commodore.
Kirk was sure of that.

He also knew he would have to talk to Spock
about his reactions to Dr. Tremain, and Kirk was more
than slightly disturbed at how much pain Spock must
have suffered on finding out that his idol had feet,
thighs, and hips of clay—and, when it came to Vulcans, a clay head as well. Sighing, Kirk signaled the
Bridge and asked Spock to join him in his, Kirk's,
quarters.

The Vulcan had known what the topic of conversation would be from the moment he entered the Captain's cabin; Kirk could read that much in his First
Officer's stiff posture and coldly controlled facial muscles. Spock was prepared to be very, very Vulcan, and
no amount of prodding would change his position.

"Well, what do you make of Tremain's prejudice,
Spock? Does it bother you as much as it does me?" It
was the wrong question; Kirk could tell that the instant
he said it. The unfortunate linking of his feelings to
Spock's could only result in the Vulcan denying any
such comparison.

"I admit to being somewhat disappointed in Dr.
Tremain, and I am puzzled as to Commodore Stone's
motives in sending her to us. But as for it *bothering*
me, Captain, I assure you that I do not allow myself
to be unduly distressed by the odd mental quirks likely
to appear in almost any Terran."

"But how are you going to react to more of her
nonsense—and what about Arachnae? You two will
have to be working together down there, you know,
and this won't make it any easier."

"I will manage to restrain myself no matter what
Dr. Tremain does. Her behavior can have no effect on

me. Also I am somewhat interested in studying her anti-Vulcan prejudice at close range. It's really quite fascinating."

Kirk was less than sure that Spock was telling him the complete truth. He had known only too well how much the presence of Dr. Tremain had meant to the Vulcan, and how eagerly he had been awaiting her arrival. But there was no point in continuing a discussion of the matter with Spock. He had obviously decided what his official position was with regard to Tremain, and Kirk knew that his First Officer would not admit to anything else happening behind his slanting eyebrows and calm Vulcanoid eyes.

"All right, Spock, I guess we'll all just have to muddle through somehow. We always do, no matter what the universe throws at us."

"But Captain, you cannot blame the universe for something that is happening inside Dr. Tremain's mind—that would be illogical."

With a weary wave of his hand, Kirk dismissed the First Officer and watched him leave the room, stiff-backed. He, Kirk, was in no mood for logic.

His problem was that he was responsible not only for the physical welfare of his crew, but also for their mental welfare as well. On a ship the size of the *Enterprise* it was easy to keep two crewmen apart who disliked one another. But officers were another matter, particularly if both wore the blue uniform of the Science section. Kirk knew it would be next to impossible to keep Spock and Tremain apart. He could only hope that the woman would have enough good sense not to blather to the crew about her hatred of Vulcans. It would be too easy to cause a situation where the crew would take sides. Spock was respected, but not beloved. Dr. Tremain was an attractive woman, and that was a powerful weapon.

Kirk could only shake his head in wonderment at his own stupidity at thinking for one moment that a captain's job could ever be easy.

The medical exam went quite well. Dr. Tremain was in excellent health, a fact Dr. McCoy had been sure of before he began the examination. But such examinations were Star Fleet requirements and an excellent safety factor for all aboard the ship. Contagious diseases could be swiftly detected before they became a problem, and it gave the ship's doctor a working familiarity with a new crewmember before he or she might require medical attention.

Nurse Christine Chapel assisted with the examination, and it was apparent to McCoy that she had already been informed of Dr. Tremain's views on Vulcans. She was coldly brisk, efficient, and said as little as possible to Tremain. McCoy decided that he must have a talk with his nurse as soon as possible. Her attitude was just short of insolence, and that could not be allowed in dealing with a superior officer.

Chapel walked away from the table to get a tray of instruments, and Tremain watched her rigid retreat with some amusement. "Doesn't like me very much, does she?" Tremain commented in a loud stage whisper. "I do hope she has a good reason for it."

"She likes Spock, and she feels she's defending him in this way. I'll have a talk with her about it after I finish here."

"Don't bother, Len. A little honest hatred is good for the soul. If it makes her feel like a champion of truth and justice, let her do it. I don't mind. But have you told her she's a fool for loving a Vulcan? And I *can* tell that she loves him; that much anger has to be from more than merely 'liking' him. It won't get her anywhere; they can't love back, you know. I'd bet my last credit that he doesn't respond worth a damn, no matter what she does for him."

Tremain was watching the reactions, or lack thereof, which Chapel was allowing her to see. There were few surface clues as to what the nurse was feeling, and Tremain felt oddly proud of her. She was sure Chapel was a very skilled nurse. It took skill to pretend she had not heard a word of the conversation.

"Christine? Let's get this finished," McCoy said, wanting the goading of his nurse to stop. "I want to get to the psychiatric sections so we can see what makes this lady tick." He winked at Tremain, and she grinned back.

"Now who's changing the topic of conversation, Doctor? But I warn you, the tests won't work. All you'll find out is that I don't like Vulcans. I had a normal childhood and my potty training was excellent, thank you. I don't want to talk about my problems with Vulcans—not to you *or* your damn machines—and that is the bottom line on the whys, and wherefores of Katalya Tremain." Her face was alight with impish joy; clearly she was enjoying the game hugely.

"It would be so much simpler if you would try to talk about it," McCoy said. "Then we could get on to a few things we'd find a great deal more interesting."

"Yes, but if I did that—if I could—it would be like Hamlet killing his uncle in the first act—we'd have no drama to deal with, no more clever lines, and it wouldn't be any fun for the audience."

"Now you're teasing me! Is that any way to treat your doctor, Dr. Tremain?" McCoy was very willing to play her game. It might give him some insight, and it might make her care for him a bit more. Professionalism was warring with his gonads, and it was going to be a neck-and-neck race as to which side won.

"I have to do that, Len. If I don't play games like this, I'd only end up crying again." Her face was pale, and a thin film of sweat formed over her forehead. "Do you think I do this for my own amusement? It's not funny, living inside my head. Day after day, feeling the thoughts pile up on each other. Oh, I'm sane enough." She looked up to see what reaction she was getting from McCoy. "I take pride in that. A twisted sort of pride. I can prove how sane I am once you start the silly tests. My sanity is not the point. The pain and horror I put up with is what matters. Do you have any idea of how dreadful it is for me every time I try to get even a little bit close to my feelings about Vulcans?

"My mind wants to vomit from the sickness of my own thoughts and make me free of them. It's like ground glass. And the nightmares! Row on row of pointy-eared beasts, and they are all after me. They want my soul—my very soul's approval of them—and they can't have it!" Her voice took on a carefully calculated note of hysteria. "I won't let them win, I can't, my mind is at stake here, and I will not let them win it!"

She turned her head away so that Chapel could not see her face as the nurse returned to the examining table.

Tremain was shaking with the agony of her own words. Her body dripped sweat onto the sheet under her, and McCoy watched with growing interest as the woman worked her way through the fit of terror mixed with hate.

"Save that for the tests. We'll run you through a Sigmund, and you'll feel a lot better." He kept his voice deliberately professional.

Chapel glanced at McCoy, and then down at Tremain. She lifted one eyebrow and said nothing.

Tremain was laughing bitterly. "Do you really think that will help? Would you care to speculate how many times I've been Sigmunded in the past year? Even I've lost track of the number. But I am sane. That's the irony of all this. I am as coldly, logically sane as any Vulcan, and I wish I weren't. Logic! How ridiculous it all is. And how hard I've tried to give it up."

"But the Vulcans didn't invent logic," Chapel said, reaching out to hold Tremain's shoulder firmly to the table. Her voice had gentled somewhat, and she was at least speaking directly to the exobiologist.

Tremain reached out a hand to Chapel and smiled. She had gotten the woman to react to her, and that was what she had wanted; McCoy was sure of that.

"You're right," Tremain said in a shaky whisper, gripping Chapel's hand. "They didn't invent it. But oh, my God, how they force it on all of us!" She let go of Chapel and relaxed on the examining table. She was smiling, and looked triumphantly pleased with the result of her outburst.

McCoy resisted the urge to applaud. The woman had done a masterful job of saying nothing while seeming to reveal a great deal. It would have been very easy to call her on the game, but McCoy's feelings for her as a desirable woman were still in conflict with his duties as a doctor. He picked up the tray of instruments and finished the rest of the physical in silence. It seemed the best thing to do at the time. He would have another crack at her once he got her into the Sigmund booth. The results of that test might be very interesting.

The concept of psychoanalyzing a newcomer to a starship was almost as old as Star Fleet. The High Command had found out the hard way that a ship's crew was a very carefully constructed gestalt, a pattern of interlocking personalities. One person, one idea, could change the shape of that whole gestalt. Sometimes such change was for the better; sometimes it could tear a crew apart, turning the ship into a chaotic battlefield of warring emotions.

Therefore, each new crew member must be scrutinized for possible catalyst factors. And no more dangerous a catalyst existed than hatred or racial bigotry.

Katalya Tremain was a walking time bomb as far as the *Enterprise* was concerned. But Star Fleet had sent her precisely to that ship because she was the best person for the job at hand. It was McCoy's duty to integrate her mental processes as carefully as possible into the processes of the ship, with as little harm as possible to both Tremain and the *Enterprise*.

The psychoanalytic machine known as "Sigmund" was a small, womblike room painted in soft

pinks. There was only enough area in it for a couch
and a computer. The ceiling was quite low, and curved
downward at the corners to accentuate the womb quality. The room had been soundproofed; Tremain
would hear nothing but the voice of the computer. She
would be made comfortable and drugs would be ad-
ministered at McCoy's discretion to aid in probing
into the recesses of her mind.

The first part of the test would be simple: questions concerning her background, her likes and dislikes, her childhood. Then it would proceed into part
two, which was a battery of questions and responses
that would uncover her basic mental attitudes, her neuroses, large and small, and the various forms of mental
luggage carried by the subconscious.

But it was the third part of the test that McCoy
was the most interested in. This was the scriptbreaker
—the probing deep into areas that not even the subject could reach. The place of blocks and mental walls.
The black pit that every man or woman carried
deep within himself. The small still voice that said with
cold honesty precisely what the person was.

McCoy would handle that part of the exam himself. He would ask the questions and watch the results.
With any luck, or skill, on his part, Katalya Tremain
would be peeled like an onion, every layer clear and
distinct. And she would fight it. She had given him
warning of that.

Tremain entered the booth gaily, almost giggling
in anticipation. McCoy knew that she was so sure of
her ability to resist that she considered this a game as
well. But he was determined to get to the bottom of
her hatred of Vulcans, and part three just might do it
—if he asked the right questions.

Nurse Chapel made Tremain comfortable on the
couch, and adjusted the automatic hypospray on her
arm that would feed the required drugs into her system.
Everything was set for the Sigmund section of Tremain's physical. McCoy had only to push a button
and the process would begin. But he hesitated.

The next few hours would tell him perhaps more about this woman than he really wanted to know, and she might come out of it hating him. One of the first rules of good Sigmunding was that, if you removed something from a patient's mind you must have something of equal value to replace it with—and McCoy did not as yet have anything that would serve as a fair exchange.

It would take time and study to determine exactly what this woman needed to replace her hatred. McCoy was almost hoping that it might be himself; but he knew full well that a casual affair would not be enough and that his thoughts were straying into dangerously unprofessional areas.

"Is she set in there?" he asked Chapel. "If so, I want to doublecheck a few things about her husband's death while she's undergoing phase one and two."

"But doctor, you *know* she was faking that outburst! I was so mad I could've shaken her for it. Playing games over something as important as a Sigmund." Chapel's indignation was, McCoy knew, due as much to her feelings about Spock as any sense of outrage at being the butt of Tremain's little game.

"I know she was faking, you know it, but does *she* know it as well? That's what one and two will tell us. As for three, I want to have a few facts on hand to hit her with where she leasts expects them. I don't want to spend my time dithering on about her supposed hatred of Vulcans. . . ."

"Then that's not real either!" There was indignation in Christine's voice.

"Oh, it's real enough, but it's a cover for something a lot deeper. Katalya Tremain doesn't have the earmarks of the conventional bigot. It doesn't sit well on someone that intelligent. But it does make a convenient excuse for whatever it is she doesn't want to admit to anyone—including herself. I'm going to find out what it is."

McCoy checked the computer readout one more

time on the Sigmund booth, found it working as pro-
grammed, and then walked to the computer terminal
on his desk.

"Give me a readout on the facts concerning the
death of Katalya Tremain's husband," he instructed
the machine. "I suspect that's where a lot of it is hidden, Christine—ah *ha!*"

The computer had been quietly nattering away in
the background, and one fact stood out from all the
rest. the captain of Jeremy Tremain's ship, *Calypso*,
had been a Vulcan named Selik.

5

Question 1: What is your race?
   a) What is (are) the race(s) of your parents?
   b) Where were you born?
Question 2: At what age did you decide to enter the Space Academy?
   a) Did your family unit approve?
   b) At what age did you enter the Academy?
   c) Was it the Academy branch closest to your home world?
   d) If not, why not?
Question 3: What was your first mission in space, and what was the name of your first ship?
   a) What was your relationship with the captain of that ship?
   b) What was your relationship with the crew?
   c) Why did you leave that ship?
Question 4: How many ships have you served on?

—Excerpts from Sigmund Program, part one

The fact that the captain of the *Calypso* had been a Vulcan came as no great surprise to McCoy. He had almost been expecting it. He would, in fact, have been disappointed with anything else. The story of that ship's last flight, though, made fascinating reading.

33

The *Calypso* had been a scout ship of the Hermes class, with a crew of nearly two hundred. Selik, its captain, had served with distinction in Star Fleet for four decades. On its last exploratory voyage, to the planet Bellaea, it had inadvertently taken aboard a small colony of parasitical creatures. Under conditions as they existed on Bellaea, these parasites were relatively harmless. But in the environment of the spaceship, they flourished with unbelievable success.

The parasites did not attack the crew directly; instead, they fed off the instruments and the machinery within the ship. So quickly did they breed, and so subtle was the damage they created initially, that they were not discovered until too late. All hell began breaking loose unexpectedly aboard the *Calypso*.

Ship functions began to fail in random patterns. In some places the parasites actually ate through the metal walls, exposing some compartments to the vacuum of space. Elsewhere, death was equally abrupt as the life-support systems began going out. Captain Selik was in the unenviable position of having his ship literally falling apart beneath him. He had lost all but the bare emergency power, and even that was fading. All his instruments were unreliable. The computer functions were suspect. And his was the ultimate decision to make.

Being a Vulcan, he made it on purely logical grounds. By his best estimate, the ship had slightly more than twenty-six hours of oxygen left, and almost no power. At the last report, there had been no other ships in his immediate area; even if the *Calypso* still had the power to send out an emergency distress signal, there was absolutely no chance of any rescue attempt reaching them in time. And even if a rescue ship were to reach them, there was the definite possibility that the parasites aboard the *Calypso* might infect the rescue ship as well, spreading further through the Galaxy.

Looked at in those terms, Captain Selik decided that, rather than subject his crew to a pointless, lingering death, he would blow the ship up, destroying the parasites in the process. Accordingly, he recorded his final command decision on tape and shot it away in a message pod, then lowered the shields between the matter and antimatter pods of the drive, utterly destroying the *Calypso* and all hands aboard.

Captain Selik had had no way of knowing that the heavy cruiser *Republic*, having suffered minor damage in an ion storm, would come past his position within twenty-two and a half hours. But perhaps it would not have mattered. A thorough investigation of the affair was conducted by Star Fleet, and the committee totally absolved Captain Selik of any culpability; it even awarded him a posthumous Medal of Honor for his actions. The incident was considered closed—by everyone, apparently, except Katalya Tremain.

McCoy suspected, however, that her hatred of Vulcans was a coverup for something deeper. The very fact that she claimed not to be able to get near those feelings proved his hypothesis that there was something more than just surface bigotry involved. But just what it might be he was not willing to speculate on as yet. He had an idea that it might revolve around her marriage—she had told him a bit about it in her cabin —but that, too, might have been as calculated as her outburst in Sick Bay. McCoy was a firm believer that one burst of hysteria might be chance, two were suspicious, and three . . . three were downright incriminating.

His job, clearly, was not stopping Tremain from hating Vulcans—although that would have to come about in time—but making her stop using hysteria as a weapon every time someone got too close to what she was thinking. Outbursts like those she'd had today could not be tolerated on board a ship like the *Enterprise*. If Tremain had been assigned to the ship on a permanent basis, McCoy would have determined that she was unsuitable and demanded her removal for the good of the ship.

But this drastic action was not needed since she

was only assigned to a limited, but very necessary, mission. Professionally he could not allow her to stay on board one minute longer than her job called for, so he would have her off the ship as soon as some decision had been made about the intelligence of the Arachnians. That was an unfortunate thing for him to cope with as a man, but for the moment the doctor in him had won, and he was sadly glad of it. It would make his job easier if he did not clutter up his mind with thoughts of desire for Katalya. If he was to help her, and his ship, he must take that attitude or he had no right being in the position he held.

He busied himself with filling out a chart on Dr. Tremain and putting in some sort of order all the information he had on her to date. She had come from a third generation Star Fleet family with a long history of loyalty to the Federation; she had numerous science awards to her credit, and there was no prior history of mental disturbance in her record. *So far, so good,* McCoy thought. *Nice and normal, just as I suspected.*

He glanced idly at the computer printout on the Sigmund and noted that she had reached the section dealing with family relations. He noted a close-knit familial pattern, a great deal of love and respect for her parents, and an interesting lack of siblings. It was something to keep in mind. Only-children of parents often reassigned to deepspace ships sometimes had problems with loneliness—and Katalya Tremain did strike him as being a very lonely woman. Her quick renunciation of the relationship with Commodore Stone bespoke a situation in which she might find it hard to form lasting attachments. McCoy knew he would have to pay close attention to the section on love and sex, which would be hitting the computer at any minute.

"Christine, let me know if you find anything interesting going on in section 1-34 through 1-57, will you? Look for abnormalities in one-to-ones. I suspect she has problems there."

"It's coming up now, and I think you're right. Come and have a look at her." Christine had been carefully monitoring the vital signs board and had noticed a jump in Dr. Tremain's pulse and blood pressure. "Something's got her really keyed up here, Doctor."

McCoy came over to his nurse's side and watched the life-sign indicators with interest. "Get me a matching readout; I want to know what's causing that."

Chapel quickly readjusted the computer screen in front of the viewing window and backspaced it to the time when Tremain's agitation had begun.

It was, as McCoy suspected, in the 1-34 to 1-57 range, and seemed to be more a problem with relationships than with sex. Tremain apparently had problems allowing herself to love anyone too deeply. The situation seemed to be fairly recent. He suspected that if he tied in the dates of her marriage with the info being presented, the figures would match. McCoy yawned. It was oh, so very simple. Like so many women before her, Katalya Tremain had been disappointed in love and was now unwilling to risk it again out of fear of losing another love object. Nothing to pay too much attention to, after all. McCoy drifted away from the computer and went back to his detailed filling in of Tremain's chart. He would wait for part two of the Sigmund before getting his hopes up again.

An hour later Nurse Chapel said, "Doctor, the first part of the Sigmund is over. Do you want a complete readout?" Chapel had been watching the screen and noting Tremain's answers, but it was impossible to tell from the woman's face what impact they might have had.

"Anything else that's interesting in there?" McCoy moved up behind his nurse and stared down at the screen.

"Not much. Standard stuff so far. Her family life was happy, no sign of bigotry there. And as she said, no problem with potty training."

"We'll know a bit more when we get to part two, but I want to know more about her assignments, both before and after her husband's death."

Christine made the necessary adjustments in the Sigmund program. "Do you want any special notation of Vulcans she might have come in contact with? That might be a good place to start."

"And exactly what she expects of us. No, I'm going to try a different tack. Get me everything you can about her marriage. Use the Sigmund subheading M2 through M25. That should turn up an interesting fact or two."

McCoy went back to the other terminal and continued his perusal of the events leading to the destruction of the *Calypso*. He learned a few facts, but nothing that gave him anything he didn't already suspect.

Katalya Tremain was going to be a hard nut to crack, but cracking her wasn't really his job. He was planning to take the Sigmund far enough to give him some idea of how to stop her erratic behavior and keep her from being too much of a bother to the *Enterprise*. And he had to work out some way to keep her on good terms with Spock—if he could ever get her to a state where the expression "good terms" might be applicable. First he had to make her acknowledge the fact that she had to work with Spock. It wasn't going to be easy, and she would fight him all the way. But McCoy did have one ace up his sleeve: Captain Kirk.

Kirk had the right to order Tremain to work with Spock or face a court-martial. He had the power to make that order stick, and Tremain knew it. Bottom line—Tremain would work with Spock. But McCoy was going to do his damnedest to make it as easy as possible on the woman. He owed her that much. And if he could achieve a breakthrough, get her over her phobia—well, a biology expert like Tremain could be very useful to the *Enterprise*.

McCoy ruthlessly suppressed that thought.

While waiting for the next part of the Sigmund to finish, McCoy treated two bruised crewmen who had tangled with a recalcitrant air pump rotor, and a lab technician with a hangnail. The cases would never achieve notice in the annals of medical history, but they were time consuming. It was almost two hours before he could again check on the progress of Tremain's Sigmund.

Sigmund Two was rolling to a stop, and McCoy took a moment or two to check the computer's opinion of her state of mind. The correlations of the machine fit nicely with his own. He was not going to waste time on a wild Vulcan chase. That would have to wait until he could offer Tremain a fair exchange for her phobia.

"Part three, here we come!" he said to Chapel. "And I'm going to put a stop to those hysterics of hers or give up my license to practice medicine. Not that I can do it all at once," he hastily amended his statement. "But I think I can get her to the point where we can all breathe a little easier around here." McCoy looked into the Sigmund room and saw that Tremain was relaxed, her eyes closed—and waiting for him to begin part three.

"Up the dexi-penithal a bit, Christine, and stand by with anphedrin if we need to bring her out of it quickly." Christine nodded her understanding of his orders and McCoy, with one backward glance and a twisted smile for his nurse, walked into the Sigmund chamber.

Tremain did not open her eyes. She simply waited.

McCoy sat down on the stool he had pulled out from under the small couch. He was at the head of the couch, looking down at the woman. Bracing himself against the wall, he prepared mentally for the fight he knew he might have on his hands very soon if he handled the situation badly.

"I know you're faking the hysteria, Katalya," he said in a deceptively soft voice. "Now, do you want to tell me why you do it?"

There was a sharp intake of breath from Tremain. Her mind had obviously not been ready for that question.

"I . . . I . . ." She took a deep breath. "It stops the pain," she said slowly. "It makes it go away. And then I feel better." Her voice sounded very young and childlike. "I don't like being asked questions I don't like. Crying and getting mad makes people stop asking those questions."

"Very good." McCoy knew he was on the right track. The childlike answers made it quite clear that he was on a very deep level indeed. It was entirely possible that the use of hysteria was nothing new as a weapon for Tremain. She had probably used it as a child, and had gotten her own way with it more than once. McCoy doubted she was even aware that she had established a pattern.

When Tremain was awake and undrugged, the hysteria probably seemed very real to her indeed. When confronted by a problem that she could not deal with, she used the very same method that had worked as a child. The doctor knew full well that the mind would return, time and time again, to a system of thought, no matter how unwise or illogical, that gave the desired result.

"Do you know, when you are awake, that the hysteria is not real?" He knew the answer, but he wanted to see what she would say.

The question seemed to throw her into a brief state of panic. It was clear she had not thought about the differences that might be present in the levels of her mind. "No, it just makes things better. Just happens, that's all. I don't think about it first."

"You upset a lot of people around you when you have hysterics."

Tremain smiled slyly; her facial expression was that of a three-year-old. "I know that. Why do you think I do it? It's very effective."

"You're saying that part of you knows how to do it, even if the rest of you does not."

"Yes. I think so." Her voice was getting drowsy, and McCoy signaled Chapel to cut down the dexi-peni-thal.

"Don't you think there might be a better method to get your own way? I can think of several. Now, what do you think of this—every time you feel like having hysterics, why don't you come and talk it over with me?"

"What if you're not in Sick Bay? You could be asleep, you know."

"Well, you could talk to Sigmund about it, and then as soon as I'm back on duty we can discuss it together. But you must come to me and talk instead of having hysterics. Is that clear?"

"Yes."

"And while you're on board the ship, I want you to avoid the Vulcan as much as possible. You know you *must* work with Spock, but when you're not around him, pretend he doesn't exist; and when you must be in his company, carry on what conversation is necessary for professional reasons, but maintain a strictly neutral attitude."

During his instructions, Tremain's face was rapidly changing from the childlike expression to her more mature self. "Will you do that for me?" McCoy finished coaxingly.

"Yes, if it's what you wish. I think I can manage it." Her voice was mature and very aware of what he was saying.

Transference of responsibility to the psychiatrist was a very old technique and, in Tremain's case, the most practical thing to do at the moment. In time he would have to wean her away, and that would be hard on him as a man, but it would help her to help herself. The Vulcan hatred could wait until he could talk her into more Sigmunding. But it was all so transparently fake he could see no real purpose in working on it now.

McCoy knew he could go on and cover a great deal more of the territory of her mind, but he had achieved his main goal of stopping, temporarily, the hysterics. There were several questions he wanted to ask about her marriage, but he felt that those, too, could wait. She did not seem to have the same reaction to discussing her marriage that she did to discussing Vulcans. There should be no problem in getting her to accept more Sigmunding in the future.

"Now you'll wake up slowly, and you'll be just fine. Just remember that, when you have hysterics, you must come and talk to me." McCoy got up slowly from the stool and reached over to remove the hypo from her arm. He hoped his makeshift patching of her mind would work long enough for him to get more done with her. She would still hate Spock, but she would not be as noisy about it.

He was sure he had ended any problems for the *Enterprise,* and that there would really be no difficulty between Tremain and Spock.

He was wrong.

6

Captain Kirk, Spock, and McCoy sat facing each other in the Briefing Room. On the central computer screen, the results of Katalya Tremain's Sigmund were winding down to the final minutes of part three. Kirk watched intently, Spock looked merely bored, and McCoy grinned like the proverbial cat in the cream factory.

"There," McCoy said gleefully as the tape finished, "you see? I have proved that she doesn't really hate Vulcans for their own sake, and she's using bigotry as a red herring to keep people away from what's really bothering her. The case is almost solved, and I'm the man to do it. I'll have that woman so well in six weeks that not even Commodore Stone will recognize her!"

"I hope you're right," Kirk answered. "We can't afford any problems with her when she and Spock go down to the surface to communicate with the Arachnians. She does know she'll be working with Spock, doesn't she?"

"She knows. I've taken care of that, too." McCoy was positively jubilant. "I've assigned myself to the landing party. I'll be with them every step of the way. There will be no problem, I can promise you that."

"I tend to disagree with you, Doctor, but that is nothing new." Spock had been listening to McCoy

43

sounding off about his success, and felt it was time to add a cautionary note. "You have done nothing to end her reactions to Vulcans, or rid her of her hatred. You have not even approached the problems you say are there concerning her marriage. All you have done is calm down her reaction to the sight of a Vulcan. Or, to be more correct, you claim to have achieved this. We have yet to see any proof of it. I believe that you have hardly touched her dislike, and have done *nothing* to end it."

"But you're wrong; I've proved it's all a fake—a feint—to keep her doctors away from what's really bothering her."

"Illogical. You will find that at the bottom of her mind there is some deep and very real feeling about Vulcans. She would not seize on such a device unless there was some validity to her beliefs."

"Look, Spock, who's got the psychiatric degree around here, you or me? I know this woman, and I know that she's only using the fact that a Vulcan was captain of the ship her husband died on as an excuse."

"And both her parents as well?" Spock's voice never changed in tone as he dropped his bombshell into the conversation. "You did not study the records very thoroughly, Doctor." Spock was enjoying the expression of shocked amazement on McCoy's face. "Or else you would have known that Science Officer Carlyle was Dr. Tremain's father, and that Dr. Alice Carlyle, Ship's Medical Officer, was her mother. I checked those facts myself this afternoon. I, too, suspected a Vulcan captain on the *Calypso,* but I did not stop my investigation the moment I had found what I was looking for. That is the difference in our methods. I do not allow myself to make that sort of mistake." Spock managed to sound smug even without any sign of emotion in his voice.

The result of the information on Dr. McCoy was astonishing. He cursed himself for six kinds of a fool, questioned his own professionalism and that of the Sigmund's programmer, and glared at Spock, daring him to say anything—anything at all.

Spock merely lifted one eyebrow and waited for the doctor to finish his tirade. He had made his point and, logically, he had nothing further to say. He had proved that Katalya Tremain had a very good reason for hating Vulcans: her parents' deaths as well as her husband's. Not a logical reason, but a reason. That was enough for him.

Any fancy mental footwork from McCoy about how he was trying to prove that hate wasn't hate but something else was just so much foolishness. Spock was not a firm believer in human psychoanalysis. He had found in the past that most of it seemed to be for the purpose of keeping the patient sick—and continuing to see his analyst. Not very logical.

Adding a machine like Sigmund changed nothing. The techniques were still the same as in the dark ages of Freud's day.

"Then it sounds as if we still have a problem," Kirk said gloomily. "I'm disappointed in you, Bones. I thought you really had solved it. Now we're back to square one. Katalya Tremain hates Vulcans."

"Yes, but there has got to be more to it than that." McCoy hastily leaped at a chance to prove himself at least partially correct. "She plays too many games about hating Vulcans for it to be real, and I did prove that the hysteria was fake."

"Then there is the possibility that both of you are right?" Kirk asked.

Spock nodded. "Quite possible, Captain. But it is also possible that we are both wrong. We have insufficient data at this time."

"Marvelous. Simply marvelous." Kirk buried his face in his hands. "We have trouble with the Romulans, a question about intelligent life that could cause a major war, and on top of that you can't even tell me a simple fact about Dr. Tremain's feelings. I think I'll go back to studying the charts on the ion storm. At least I can understand them."

Spock and McCoy were reluctantly forced to agree with the Captain. They had no clearcut answer about Tremain.

McCoy hurried back to his office to reread the entire Sigmund again. He had ended the process rather quickly, he now admitted. He had been in such a rush to show his results to Kirk and Spock that he had not really followed through on the evidence. He had dismissed Tremain, telling her that he would continue her indoctrination the next day, and then called Kirk into the Briefing Room with, as he now saw, disastrous results. Technically he had no right to ask permission for another Sigmund after dismissing her from the first one unless she agreed to it—and, in his haste, he had not asked for such assurances. He now had no contract with her for any further Sigmunding.

McCoy cursed himself for letting the opportunity get away from him. If she refused more Sigmunding, he would have to prove to the satisfaction of a Star Fleet board of inquiry that there was some real need to order her into continuing analysis. He'd pushed himself even further into a corner of his own making by trying to stop the hysterics that were the main form of outward expression of her feelings. If she no longer had the hysterics, he couldn't claim that they were interfering with her work sufficiently to make further Sigmunding necessary. Until she exhibited some abnormalities of a sufficiently dangerous nature, his hands were tied.

He slowly reread the Sigmund and grumbled at his own incompetence. There had been some questions about the deaths of her parents. But they were mostly related to how the patient felt about the possibility of his or her own death, so they were of little help in saying how Tremain felt about her parent's deaths. He made a note to amend the Sigmund program and that he would have to report the failure of the test to the Star Fleet med corps. The fact that the Sigmund was partially at fault was small comfort. His only hope now was getting her cooperation for more tests, or picking up what clues he could from observing her behavior in the time that would elapse before the *Enterprise* reached Arachnae.

One week was a very short time indeed to find out anything. By her own admission Tremain had been examined by several doctors, and they had been unable to do anything about her prejudice or the underlying emotions that McCoy was sure had to be there.

The next morning McCoy continued Tremain's indoctrination by taking her through the life science labs and introducing her to personnel. She was suitably impressed by the care that had been taken to keep the labs in perfect ready condition and by the high morale of the people involved.

It was not a group that sat around and got bored waiting for something to happen. Discipline was good, but not so tight as to be restrictive, and the general feeling of the labs was one of calm purpose. Tremain liked that very much. It fit very well with her own attitudes toward her life's avocation. In these rooms she was a pure bright flame of scientific reason; biological investigation was her justification for living.

She caressed a tabletop and, eyes gleaming, complimented McCoy on the way he kept his labs. "I like it here," she said. "I could be very happy spending the rest of my life in rooms like these."

"It would make me happy, too. Having you here, I mean."

"Even after yesterday?" she asked. "I know that the Sigmund was a failure—your face told me that this morning. You seemed so pleased with yourself when you dismissed me after the test. What happened?"

"I ran amok chasing after a red herring that I had invented on my own, and I got properly called down for it by the Captain."

"And the Science Officer," she added. "I bet he enjoyed that a lot. Vulcans generally do like catching one in error."

"You could help me prove he's wrong by letting me Sigmund you again and letting me get all that stuff out at once," he said, hoping she'd take the bait.

Tremain grinned, showing her teeth in a fox-like smile. She'd seen the trap only too easily. "No way. I won't let you play hunt and peck on my mind just because you want to score on the Vulcan. You'll have to get another reason to get me back in there. And it had better be one that will stick with the Star Fleet board of inquiry. I've given you the one Sigmund Star Fleet regulations entitle you to, and that's all you're going to get. You have no right to put me back into that room without my permission. By Star Fleet definition I'm not neurotic. The major test of a neurosis is whether I can function properly within the bounds of my job classification without interference from my own private reality. I can, and you know it; you even helped me by working out a way to deal with my hysteria."

"How did you know about that?"

"Simple. I used my 'need to know' coding for the Sciences section and read the whole Sigmund. It was quite interesting. Not very accurate. As you said, it was nothing more than a red herring—but a good one, I admit. Next time, remember to lock files like that if you don't want most of the Science section, or me, to be reading it. But then, if you do lock it I'll have a good idea that you think you're onto something, and that won't make your job any easier; I'll see to that."

"But what about your marriage—talking about your husband? Will you do that without a Sigmund?"

"Oh, I'll talk about my husband until the cows come home. It was a rotten marriage, that's all. You will not find anything interesting there that will help you. I have no hidden corners when it comes to Jeremy Tremain. But even if we talk about Jeremy, that still doesn't give you the right to Sigmund me again. We have no contract allowing you to take possession of my mind."

McCoy sighed. Between the Vulcan and this woman, he was sure that any ideas he might develop about her problem would be ground into tiny bits of nothing, smelling to high heaven of red herring. It was a game he was not likely to win—for this round, at least.

"Well, just let it go for now." He gave in gracefully, knowing he was beaten. "But I give you warning, at the first sign of something I think will stick with the review board, you'll be in there so fast your id will swim." He walked toward the door to the outside corridor, saying over his shoulder, "Let's get on with the rest of the indoctrination, Katalya, there are some people I want you to meet. Particularly there's a woman in the Veterinary Lab across the hall that you'll be working with on the surface, and you should get to know her now."

The Veterinary Lab had at one time been an extra doctor's office, but after problems with alien animals such as tribbles, it was felt necessary to have an extra section devoted exclusively to animal studies. The room was small and made even smaller by the confusion of cages which filled every available corner, stacked one on top of another up to the ceiling. There was an examining table, several cabinets filled with equipment, and an incredible clutter of files taking up what little room remained. The smell was abominable, and the sound of fifty different animals from as many planets chattering, shrieking, and yelling filled the air with an almost impossible din.

"Ruth," McCoy called out, "are you in here?" He peered behind a row of cages. "I've got to get her a larger room," he muttered to himself. "Heaven knows she works hard enough to deserve it. . . ."

"Over here," a gentle voice called as the door to the washroom opened. The woman entering the room was a small, heavyset blonde with the face of a Michelangelo madonna. Most of her rather well-rounded body was hidden from view by the large mongcat she was carrying. The lavender-striped animal was clinging to the front of her uniform with all six of its tiny humanlike hands, and its prehensile tail was wrapped securely around the lieutenant's waist. It was wailing in a highpitched voice, and the veterinarian turned to comfort it.

"Now, Fuzzybutt, a bath isn't that bad. Stop fussing. Come on, baby, there are guests here. Try to act nice." She smiled at McCoy and shrugged the animal up higher onto her shoulder. "He hates being disinfected," she explained sweetly. "But he hates fleas even more. I think he caught them from the sabercat; I'm not looking forward to giving *him* a bath!"

"I'll get some lab techs in to help you; you just holler when you need them. Now I want you to meet someone. Dr. Tremain, this is Dr. Ruth Rigel, Chief Veterinarian and my favorite animal lover." He smiled at the woman with genuine warmth. "Ruth, Dr. Tremain is going to be heading up the Arachnae probe."

"Oh? I thought Mr. Spock was in charge of that." She shifted the mongcat again and freed one hand to extend it to Tremain. "But I am glad to meet you—I've heard almost nothing from Spock and Dr. McCoy for the past few weeks but how excited they were that you're coming aboard."

"Thank you," Tremain shook hands with the veterinarian. "Dr. McCoy is correct, I am in charge of the probe. I'm not even sure we will need Mr. Spock's help on the surface. I spent last night going over the records of some of the tech crew, and I think we can put together an acceptable party without the Vulcan."

Rigel frowned, a gentle corrugation of her brow. "But Spock has to go along—he's the Science Officer! I did hear some rumors that you didn't like him, Dr. Tremain. But I try not to pay attention to rumors."

"They're not rumors," Tremain said coldly. "They're facts. I will not work with Vulcans."

"But he's not just any Vulcan," Rigel protested.

"He's Mr. Spock—one of the best Science Officers in the Fleet. We'll need him, I know that."

"Thank you for your opinion, Dr. Rigel, but I am in command and I will pick my own staff." Tremain's voice allowed no room for argument.

The veterinarian nodded coolly. "Come on, Fuzzybutt, we need to get you into a cage so you won't get cold." *Or contaminated by bigotry.* Her unspoken words were all too apparent to McCoy and Tremain.

7

Captain Kirk called a meeting the next day in the Briefing Room so that the principals could all become better acquainted with their mission. Ordinarily he would have had just Spock and Tremain present as the two leaders of the expedition to Arachnae; but because of the delicate situation, he asked McCoy to attend as well. That could at least be justified on the grounds that McCoy would go along with the exploratory party, too.

The tension within the room was tangibly thick. Kirk sat with Spock at his side. When Tremain entered the room and saw that, she pointedly moved down to sit at the far end of the long white table. McCoy was torn in his loyalties, but finally opted to sit next to Tremain so that she wouldn't feel completely isolated; he knew that Kirk and Spock would understand.

Kirk cleared his throat and, ignoring the charged atmosphere, began, "We'll be reaching Arachnae in about three more days. I believe that Dr. Tremain and Mr. Spock have both had time to do some preliminary studies of the problem, and I'm anxious to hear their opinions. Mr. Spock, could you give me a rundown on the planet itself?"

"Certainly, Captain. Arachnae is a Class M world, and as such it has less water than most other habitable planets. Its oceans are smaller and shallower, its rivers are narrower. Rainfall is uncommon. As a result, most of the native life has learned to adapt to drier conditions. They are hardier than, say, Terran life forms, but no less varied. The planet has approximately the same diameter and gravitational strength as Earth. The air is breathable with no known microorganisms dangerous to humanoid life forms. In short, it is a planet not unlike many others we have visited in the past."

"Good," Kirk nodded. "Then we needn't expect too many surprises from the planet itself. Its inhabitants, however, are another matter. Dr. Tremain, since this is your specialty, could you fill me in on them?"

"Very well, Captain." Tremain looked straight at Kirk as though there were no Vulcan seated beside him. Then, glancing down at her notes, she punched a button beside her place, and the computer obediently produced an image on the central screens for all to observe.

The creature on the screen looked something like a cross between an ant and a tarantula. It was covered with a golden yellow fur and moved about on six legs, the front two of which seemed more dextrous than the others. The Arachnian was also equipped with sharp mandibles that could rend its food—or practically anything else that needed rending. There was nothing else in the picture to give an indication of size, but Kirk got the impression that the creature was at least as big as a large dog, perhaps even bigger.

"As you can see, Captain, the creature is nonhumanoid in shape," Tremain said dryly. Kirk wondered whether the sarcasm was special for this occasion or whether it was her standard lecturing style. "This created special problems for the Federation scout team that reported on Arachnae."

Kirk could well believe that. Since the majority of intelligent races tended to be humanoid in appearance, the standard scouting method used by the Federation —consistent with the Prime Directive of noninterference with local development—was to disguise a number of scouts to look like the natives and have them wander about within the culture they were investigating; that way they could report on the attainments of the new society with a minimum of interference in the local culture.

Such a procedure could not have worked on Arachnae, simply because it was impossible to disguise any Federation scouts to look like Arachnians. The observers would have had to collect all their information from a distance while remaining hidden from the natives—not the optimum method at all.

"It was the ambiguity of the scouting reports," Tremain continued, "that has led to our immediate problem. The scouts observed the Arachnians in groups, apparently communicating with one another in an intelligent manner, and using tools. All of these activities *could* be signs of intelligence. But as the scouts themselves noted, there are plenty of cases where non-sentient beings have engaged in similar behavior without indicating anything of the sort. On Earth alone, ants work in groups, bees communicate to one another about the location of food, and apes use tools. Only that last group could be considered as possessing rudimentary intelligence. I would have to consider the question very much open at this point."

"You will have to admit, Doctor, that brain-case size might be a factor in this instance," Spock said. "In the terrestrial animals you mentioned, the sizes of their brains are generally too small to allow room for the development of sentient mentality. The Arachnians, however, have heads and brains almost the size of a human's. It is therefore slightly more probable that they have developed reasoning faculties."

Although Tremain clearly heard the remark, she addressed her reply to Kirk rather than directly to Spock. "There are people, Captain, who insist on equating quantity with quality. Brain size alone—or even the more reliable index of brain size ratio in comparison to body size—is no indication of intelligence. To think that it is would be to make a serious error—as serious, say, as equating knowledge with wisdom. We all know how fallacious *that* is."

Spock was about to protest, but Kirk cut him off. He had hoped that this meeting could be conducted in a rational, scientific manner, but it was obvious that Tremain's prejudices would not allow that. She was still showing some anger from the initial meeting with Spock; perhaps she needed some more time to settle into the shipboard routine. It was apparent that both had done their homework and studied the background reports; there was little to be gained by a further session of bickering.

"Well, it seems to me that you've both studied the problem, although you apparently arrived at separate conclusions. More study may be in order before we arrive. I suggest that you each do a little more thinking on your own and perhaps we can discuss it again before we reach Arachnae. I think that will be all for now."

Tremain nodded, stood up, and walked briskly out of the room, her path taking a wide arc away from Spock's position. McCoy followed a few steps after her, looking sheepishly at his commanding officer.

"You'd better see that she's a little more civilized, Bones, before we reach Arachnae," Kirk said quietly—too quietly.

McCoy could only shrug his shoulders and follow Tremain out the door.

Kirk watched him go with a profound sense of foreboding. *That woman is only going to cause more trouble before this mess is over—and it's a pity, considering how lovely she is. . . .*

The thought disturbed him, and he quashed it quickly.

Dr. McCoy, by reason of the captain's orders, found himself in the unenviable position of being both the guardian of the gestalt and the watchdog of Katalya Tremain. He was not happy with that position.

It interfered with his own pursuit of Katalya, and he found it difficult to reconcile her needs with the needs of the *Enterprise*. He found himself in the middle of an elaborate balancing act, one in which Katalya was more than willing to assist him. She had, as per his request and the captain's, ceased from any active proselytizing about Vulcans. Dr. Rigel avoided her as much as possible, and Christine Chapel maintained a polite but professional distance. The remainder of the crew, once they had gotten over the seven-days' wonder of having a Vulcan-hating officer on board, went back to their own opinions about Spock. The ship seemed peaceful.

McCoy, however, was not sure how real the peace might be. He knew very well that there were members of the ship's company who disliked the Vulcan intensely, and he was afraid they would use Dr. Tremain as a focal point. In particular, he was concerned about Ensign Lowrey.

Ensign Theodore Lowrey had been assigned to the *Enterprise* six months before as a junior science officer. The ensign had come aboard without any preconceived notions concerning Vulcans, but had very rapidly developed an intense dislike for the Science Officer. The dislike should have gone the other way. As a junior science officer, Theodore Lowrey was the most inept man ever to walk through a laboratory. It was a thing of amazement to both McCoy and Spock that the young man had even managed to graduate from the Academy. The fact that his father was Admiral Michael Lowrey may have had something to do with it. Ensign Lowrey was incapable of carrying out instructions properly, incapable of performing an experiment without utterly destroying the lab equipment, and incapable of filling out a form in any sort of coherent manner. Spock endured the young man with a thinly veiled impatience. The Vulcan was possessed of a cold, barbed style of language, which he used frequently on his junior officers. It had gotten very much under Lowrey's skin to have Spock comment acidly on each and every error, repeatedly. Every time Lowrey came up with a new mistake, Spock not only commented on that, but also reminded Lowrey of the three hundred and seventy-seven mistakes he had made before this new error.

Ensign Lowrey complained bitterly to his father, to his father's friends, and to Captain Kirk. His complaints got him nowhere. Spock put him to work washing test tubes, assuming that this would be an area where the young man would get into the least possible trouble. A hundred and fifty broken test tubes later, Mr. Spock decided that had not been the wisest of decisions. Ensign Lowrey was currently filling the position of excess baggage in the Science section, and Spock was awaiting orders from the Science Institute that would allow him to have the young man permanently removed. Ensign Lowrey, meanwhile, was forming his own clique of Vulcan haters who would help him justify his report to Star Fleet. To him, Katalya Tremain seemed ready-made to be a new member of his complaint board.

Dr. McCoy was very concerned about Ensign Lowrey and Katalya Tremain getting together. He need not have worried.

Katalya Tremain had been on board the *Enterprise* two days before she encountered Ensign Lowrey. The ensign confronted her at dinner, in one corner of a half-empty mess. He had with him three of his cronies, two young engineers and a disgruntled nurse. Ensign Lowrey requested permission to join Tremain at her table.

"This is Engineer Shigeda," he said, indicating the handsome young Oriental, "and Engineering Technician Hans Mueller." The young blond man bowed. Lowrey then introduced the nurse, Angela Dickinson, and finished by explaining that he was Theodore Lowrey, son of Admiral Lowrey.

"Oh, yes," Tremain said, indicating they could sit down. "I've heard of you, Lowrey. You're the new dunsel, aren't you?"

Lowrey blushed at the use of the Academy nickname for someone or something that is totally useless aboard a ship. "That's not my fault," he blustered. "It's that damn Vulcan. He's jealous of me. He dislikes the fact that I have important relatives. And he wants to keep me in my place. I want your help in proving that."

"I've been told that the Vulcan himself has rather important relatives," Tremain observed dryly. She was rather amused over what she recognized as the ship's delegation of Vulcan-haters. She had known that she would be approached at some time or another by such a faction, and she was fully prepared to deal with them. Her promise to Dr. McCoy, or Captain Kirk's orders, had really nothing to do with how she felt about such a group.

"We were told you didn't like the Vulcan very much, Dr. Tremain," Nurse Dickinson observed. "Christine Chapel's very mad at you, you know. But then she's so soppy in love with that Vulcan. He treats her like a retarded child and she doesn't even realize it. Oh, he's kind enough, in that condescending, cold way of his, and she eats it up. But actually she's nothing but dirt under his feet."

"And he's never looked twice at you, has he?" Tremain said sweetly.

Angela Dickinson paled, and said nothing.

"Well, Nurse, that takes care of *your* objection to Mr. Spock," Tremain observed. "Now, Mr. Shigeda, what is your position on Vulcans?"

The young man's face hardened into cold stubbornness. "I don't like them," he said. "They look funny. They smell funny. They're aliens. They're a blot, a reminder of the unclean things in this Galaxy. The Universe belongs to the Terrans. We are the strong ones. We are the deserving sons of the Universe. And humanoids blending their unclean blood with pure Terrans is something we cannot tolerate. Spock is a symbol of such mongrelization. That his not even human father dared put his hands on the pure body of a Terran—"

"Oh, you're one of *those*," Tremain said. "I've met your like before. Racial purity and all that. I had thought concepts like yours would have died out on Terra a long time ago. Most philosophers believed, the first time we realized there were other beings in the Universe, that it would unite us—that there would be less bickering about the different cultural races of Earth. It united us, all right. And in some cases, such as yours, it united us against everyone else." She then turned to Mueller. "I hope your objections are a little more sensible."

"Yes. I tend to agree with Ensign Lowrey. My objection is not to Vulcans per se, but to Commander Spock himself. The man has extraordinarily high standards of perfection, which are perfectly acceptable for a Vulcan—but he insists that all of us live up to them as well. He does not allow any room for error whatsoever. We must be absolutely perfect in everything we do or say, and I for one am getting damned sick of all that perfection."

Tremain leaned back in her chair, nodding quietly. "All right," she said, "I've heard your comments, and Lowrey I already know about. Just what do you propose to do about the Vulcan?"

The next few minutes consisted of a babble, steadily rising in volume, of complaints, comments, suggestions, and general vocal carryings-on. Tremain raised her hand for silence.

"Please, please, I can't understand it when all four of you talk at once. Lowrey, I assume you're some sort of spokesman. Would you mind telling me in detail exactly what you people have in mind? Try for a little conciseness and, if you'll pardon the expression, as little emotion as possible."

Lowrey looked at his companions and, when he got their acceptance, began to speak. "We feel that Commander Spock has no place on the *Enterprise*. We would like to see him removed. And we are in the process of drawing up a petition toward just those ends. We've been keeping careful track of his behavior for the past few months, and it is thoroughly unacceptable to any of us. As soon as we get enough material, we're not only going to have him removed from the *Enterprise* but, if we can prove it, we can have him court-martialed for nonfeasance. And that's where you come in. Dr. Tremain, you're a very important person, Spock's equal in rank, and your words count for a great deal. If you work with us and help us get rid of Mr. Spock, we would recommend that *you* be made Science Officer of the *Enterprise*."

Tremain struggled with herself not to laugh. This sort of stupidity was exactly what she had expected from such people. She looked at each one carefully, memorizing their faces and attitudes as a way of convincing herself that she was not like any of them.

"Did any of you read the reports in the computer concerning the destruction of the *Calypso?*" she asked.

The faces of the four people across from her remained blank. They had obviously not read the designated report.

"Then you obviously know nothing whatsoever about *my* quarrel with Vulcans. And since you have not even taken the trouble to read those reports, your lack of thoroughness does not impress me. What I would advise is that if you can't get along with the Vulcan then you should all transfer to other ships, because what you are suggesting borders very closely on mutiny. I do not wish to align myself with either fools or traitors. And you, my dears, fall into *both* categories."

She rose to her feet and smiled at them. "Do you have any idea what it would do to your respective careers if I were to go straight to Captain Kirk with a report of this conversation? There would be a court-martial, but it wouldn't be of Commander Spock. It would be for all of you." She turned and walked out of the room, leaving four very flabbergasted individuals behind her.

But Katalya Tremain did not report the conversation to Captain Kirk. Part of her believed that these young people were entitled to their own opinions, as long as they did not take them to a point where they would be damaging to the ship. Also, she had no wish to find herself in the middle of such a board of inquiry as a report of the conversation would cause.

Dr. McCoy very quickly received word that Lowrey and company had spoken to Dr. Tremain. But it was Nurse Dickinson, not Tremain, who told him. The young nurse did have very strong feelings about Vulcans—particularly about one Vulcan—and it wasn't hatred. She was frightened by what had happened in the mess room, and she ran to McCoy to bleat on his shoulder over the results of Lowrey's meeting with the biologist. McCoy alternately consoled and condemned the young nurse, and recommended that she follow Dr. Tremain's advice and transfer out. But he was quite relieved at the outcome of the encounter. His opinion of Dr. Tremain went up considerably.

When he spoke to her about the incident, commending the way she'd handled it, she asked why Lowrey, Shigeda, Mueller, and Dickinson were still aboard the *Enterprise* since their attitude toward Spock was a danger to the ship's gestalt. The doctor explained that both Lowrey and Mueller would be removed from the ship at the next starbase; Dickinson didn't really hate Vulcans; and Shigeda, unfortunately, was indispensable down in Engineering because of his specialized familiarity with the life support systems. Chief Engineer Scott *was* demanding Shigeda's removal, but McCoy was sure that once Lowrey was out of the way, the catalyst would be gone and Shigeda would sink back to his former obscurity. In any event, he would have little contact with Spock, so there should be no trouble.

There were still areas, though, in which Dr. Tremain's presence aboard the *Enterprise* would be a problem. One of those areas was Dr. McCoy's own Sick Bay. Christine Chapel was doing her best to hide her dislike of the newcomer, but she was not always successful.

Tremain's position as temporary ship's biologist would not generally involve her in the workings of Sick Bay. However, McCoy's growing interest in the woman, and his professional concern with the workings of her mind, did produce a situation where Tremain was in and out of Sick Bay at odd hours. Chapel was placed in a position of constant vigilance, and Dr. McCoy was of very little help. He had not confided in his nurse because he knew how she felt about Spock. He knew that her professional side would have been more than willing to help him, but it was her emotions he couldn't trust—any more than he could trust his own.

Tremain's trips to Sick Bay were primarily to see McCoy. She did respect the man, and even felt a growing liking for him, but something inside her, something cold and quiet, said, "No. This is not the right man for you." And Tremain had learned to listen to those inner voices.

Chapel's careful professional politeness also amused Tremain because she was aware of the reasons behind it. Tremain stayed away from the nurse as much as possible. She also tried to avoid Spock—but that was not always as easy as she would have liked.

Dr. Tremain was seated on one corner of McCoy's desk. McCoy sat facing her, his feet on the desk resting only centimeters from her hand. She reached out and tapped him lightly on the ankle. "Len, I don't care if you promise to do the dance of the seven veils, I will not work with that Vulcan. And I am going to find a way to avoid his participation in the Arachnae project. I had thought of seducing Kirk. Do you think that would do me any good, or would your dear Captain simply take my trembling body to his bed and then do what he damn well pleased about the Vulcan?"

"Talya, Talya, my dear, Talya. How can I explain the many ways in which I love the convoluted workings of your mind, and how I want to know more about it and your body as well, I might add."

Tremain laughed delightedly. "My dear, like your Captain you can find out anything you want to know about my sexual preferences by coming to my cabin; it isn't necessary to get me into the Sigmund. Besides, that couch is entirely too narrow and uncomfortable for most of the things I really enjoy."

McCoy grinned ruefully. He was tempted to take her up on the offer, and he knew if he did she would be more than willing. But something was holding him back. That something was his professional itch. He knew that once he allowed himself the freedom of her bed, his professionalism would be buried under several layers of emotion—and that would be very bad for both of them.

Christine Chapel walked into the office just in time to catch the last small bit of the conversation. "Doctor, you're needed in Sick Bay—a crewman has come in with a badly damaged hand, and I think several of the tendons are torn."

McCoy got to his feet, nodded to Tremain, and left the room. Nurse Chapel lingered a minute. "I hope, Doctor, that you're not becoming serious about Dr. McCoy," she said, knowing it was none of her business. "He's a very good man, and I know he cares a lot for you, but if he falls in love he's going to want you aboard this ship all the time—and that would not be good for the *Enterprise*."

Tremain looked up at the nurse. Her face was calm, considering. "Not good for the *Enterprise?*" she said. "Or for Mr. Spock? Don't worry, I have no intention of staying on this ship—and it has nothing whatsoever to do with your precious Vulcan. But I do thank you for your warning, and I will keep it in mind."

Chapel turned to go as the door to the office opened and Spock entered. The nurse froze, unwilling to leave Spock and Tremain alone.

"I have here the reports on the efficiency of the twenty-four hour use of Lab Three," Spock said, proffering the portable computer-board. "Dr. McCoy requested it."

"Dr. McCoy is with a patient at the moment," Chapel said, "but I can take care of it for you."

"Have you done any further reports on the biological makeup of Arachnae?" Tremain asked, speaking directly to the Vulcan.

Spock turned to her, surprise written boldly across his face. She had startled the Vulcan into betraying some small sign of emotion because, since she had arrived on board ship and announced her feelings about Vulcans, she had said nothing directly to him before. He quickly pulled his face back into its required formal stiffness.

"My research has revealed nothing new, and nothing that cannot already be found on the computer tapes of the previous missions. But I would be more than willing to discuss such material with you."

"No, that won't be necessary. I would prefer to listen to the computer." Dr. Tremain slid off the desk, moved around it, and sat down in McCoy's chair. She leaned forward, placing her elbows on the desk, one hand cupping her chin. She stared at Spock, taking in every Vulcan aspect of his face. Her glance traveled slowly up the inclined planes of his cheeks, tracing the abrupt slant of his eyebrows. She stared at his ears.

Spock stood quietly, allowing the examination. Embarrassed, Tremain looked away to one side.

"I still want to lead the expedition myself," she said. "I do not feel there's any need for you on the planet's surface. In fact, it might be better if you stayed on board ship and coordinated the incoming data."

"That would be inefficient, Doctor," Spock said, "and I would prefer to make my own observations. I have become somewhat convinced that the Arachnians are sentient beings, and I wish to pursue that line of thought on my own."

"Don't you trust my observations?" Tremain asked. "My specialty, in case you have forgotten, *is* exobiology. I know more about the nature of such creatures, before I've even gotten to the planet, than you would ever be able to know in years of direct study."

Spock moved over to the desk and stood facing her. He had completely forgotten the presence of Christine Chapel. "Dr. Tremain, you are being unreasonable. I am of the opinion that you have already made up your mind that the Arachnians are merely animals. It may interest you to know that my father tends to agree with you."

Tremain raised her eyebrows in a fair imitation of the Vulcan mode. "Are you attempting to utilize my dislike of your species as a means of getting me to change my mind? I really don't care what your father believes; his opinions are of no more interest to me than a belief in the existence of Santa Claus or the Tooth Fairy. There is one area where I do not allow personal prejudices to affect me, and that is my work. I am a scientist first and foremost, and I am approaching this problem from a purely scientific basis. Nothing in the previous investigations indicated anything other than a hive-life existence for these beings."

"I find it quite fascinating that we have both studied the same data and have come to completely opposite views. I hereby request that I be included in the expedition, in the interest of fairness and balance. You have, obviously, already made up your mind on the question of Arachnae before you even set foot on the planet, and I find that quite illogical," Spock commented.

Tremain smiled up at him and waited to pounce. "And *you* are illogical, Mr. Spock, for you too have formed preconceived notions about the intelligence of the Arachnians."

Spock stepped back from the desk and prepared his barrage of logical proof as to why he had not prejudged the situation on Arachnae. He did not have the chance to verbalize his proofs. Christine Chapel walked up to the desk and glared at Tremain.

"You're only trying to keep him off the expedition because you dislike him. Why don't you come out and admit that?"

Spock and Tremain looked at the nurse in some surprise. They had not expected her to enter the conversation.

"Miss Chapel, this does not concern you," both Spock and Tremain said almost in unison.

"I won't stand for it," Chapel continued. "I know what will happen when you two get down to the planet's surface. You, Tremain, will claw him apart, and he won't do a thing back because he's a Vulcan! Because he has to stay calm and logical. But you can use every bit of your emotional venom on him, and he has to stand there and accept it. Do you think that's at all fair, do you think it's right, what you're doing? If I had my way, I'd insist there would be a security guard with you at all times. I don't trust you, and I don't like the idea of your being on the planet's surface together."

"My dear, do you really think I would run the risk of trying to kill him?" Tremain steepled her fingers beneath her chin. "Although I admit the idea is rather interesting." She was being deliberately provocative.

"How dare you!" Chapel was fast losing the last vestiges of her temper. "How dare you sit there in front of him and say things like that? Don't you realize that underneath all that stoic Vulcan calm, he probably has feelings too? How can you be so vile?"

Spock was looking distinctly embarrassed. Tremain glanced first at him, and then at Chapel. "Why are you doing this?" she said softly to the nurse. "What do you think this outburst will accomplish?"

"I'll make sure he's safe from someone like you— someone who only wants to hurt him, who doesn't

understand how painful the things you say can be."
Chapel looked toward Spock for some sort of recognition of what she was doing to try to help him.
Spock said nothing; he shifted from foot to foot, decidedly uneasy with the turn the conversation was taking.

"I think you've said quite enough, Miss Chapel,"
Tremain said, rising from behind the desk. "I understand why you felt this outburst was necessary, but I do not condone it. What you're doing here does nothing whatsoever to change the basic situation between Mr. Spock and myself, and you are hurting him a great deal."

"*Me?* I'm not the one hurting him—you are!
You're the one spouting anti-Vulcan comments, you're the one talking about how much you hate Vulcans."
Chapel was trembling with rage. "If I had my way, *you* wouldn't even be allowed on the planet's surface —it would be Mr. Spock leading the expedition, not you. You'd be the one left behind to coordinate. I—I —I don't even understand why Star Fleet considers you at all useful. Your prejudices blind you to anything that matters; you can't see what is standing right in front of you—a worthwhile, intelligent being whose feelings you've badly hurt—"

"But Mr. Spock has no feelings." Tremain looked down at the desktop and brushed her fingers idly across it. "Or at least he *says* he lacks them. But either way, you are the one doing the damage."

She looked up at Chapel with an unreadable expression on her face, a mixture of emotions moving too swiftly to be catalogued accurately. "I have only one thing to say before I declare this conversation finished: If you really loved him, if you really felt a deep and abiding love for that Vulcan, you would never ever do this. Love is the cruelest gift one can give a Vulcan." Tremain, her face a mask, quickly pushed past the startled nurse and left the office by the corridor door. Spock turned to watch her leave, one eyebrow lifted, with an extremely thoughtful look on his face.

8

"Len, I'm almost beginning to like being on board the *Enterprise*." Tremain leaned her elbows against the viewing window on the observation deck and glanced over her shoulder at the doctor standing just behind her. "I'm finding this trip into deep space a great deal more enjoyable than any other I've been on. I feel like I could do this sort of thing for years."

"And even put up with a Vulcan?" McCoy reached out to turn Tremain around and take her gently in his arms. "That is the one thing you have to come to grips with, Katalya: to stay aboard the *Enterprise,* you would have to get over hating Vulcans."

Tremain frowned, creases forming across her forehead. "You would have to bring up something unpleasant like that just when I'm enjoying myself. It's not me who has a problem, it's the Vulcans. They're so thoroughly unpleasant—oh, let's not talk about it. Let's talk about something more pleasant . . . like you and me."

"But it *does* involve us," McCoy said, bending down to kiss her on the forehead. His lips brushed the furrowed skin until it smoothed. "You see, for anything serious to happen between us, you have to get over this attitude. I can't let you stay on the ship and upset the gestalt, and I can't allow my own feelings to take precedence over the safety of the *Enterprise*."

Tremain gently pushed him away and moved down the corridor the length of one more observation window. She stood staring out into deep space, watching the stars streak by. "I'm sorry, Len. I really am sorry. I like you a lot, you know. I like you enough to even want to spend the next several years of my life with you. But I don't love you that much."

"Oh, am I just another Commodore Stone, then?" McCoy started to move toward her, then stopped. "It's not a very enviable position, Katalya. What does it take to get you to care about someone?"

"I—I'm not really sure. It's been such a long time since I've loved anyone. It's not something you can will, something you can demand of yourself; it's either there or it isn't." Her voice was oddly muffled. McCoy could see that she was talking into one corner of the observation window frame.

"Hey," he said, moving closer, "I'm over here, remember? Turn around and face me while you tell me you don't love me."

"It won't change anything." She turned around slowly and faced him, her elbows resting in back of her against the window frame. "I do not love you, Leonard McCoy. I like you, I'm fond of you, I desire you. Is there anything else you wish me to say?"

"No. You're not able to say the one thing I want to hear; the rest of it means nothing. Of course, it could help if you could perhaps say one thing about possibly loving me in the future." McCoy put his arms at his side, waiting.

Tremain slid her elbows down off the window ledge and rushed toward McCoy. Grabbing him in her arms, she held him as close as possible. "Oh Len, Len, it's so complicated. If only I could make it simple for you, if only I could do exactly what you want, come out and say, 'Yes, I love you,' whether I meant it or not. But it isn't that easy. I have a lot of things to work through in my head, and so do you." She laughed shakily. "Oddly enough, we both have the same thing to work through—how we feel about Vulcans. If you want to know about love, Len—you do love him, you know. Oh, it's not the same sort of thing you feel for me," she said quickly to forestall his protests. "But there's a depth of caring, a loyalty, that I don't feel for you. And until I do, I can never say that I love you."

"Good heavens, child, we sound like a couple of doomed lovers." McCoy laughed and pulled her closer to him. "It's so silly, it sounds like a Gothic romance. This horrendous shadowy figure of a Vulcan will come between us, alas, alas."

Tremain giggled wildly, and McCoy joined her in laughter until the corridor rang with the sound of their rueful merriment.

Tremain stopped giggling and glanced up at the still-chuckling McCoy. "You know, it's nothing really to laugh about. We reach Arachnae in two days, and then the real pressure is on. There'll be you and me and a team of experts down there on that planet's surface—and there's going to be a lot of hard work. I don't want any more trouble. I'm not looking forward to the lecture I'm going to get from Captain Kirk. It's going to be such a deadly bore, and then going down there on the planet and having to face heaven knows what."

"You left out one crucial fact. Spock will be going with us. There's nothing you can do to change the Captain's orders. Spock will be with us."

Tremain frowned again, deeper creases forming, and her mouth set angrily. "I won't have it. I won't work with him. The very idea turns my stomach."

"But I'll be there with you. Remember what I taught you in the final part of the Sigmund. Whenever it gets too much, you come to me. You don't blow. You have to come to me."

"But don't you see how much easier it would be if he did stay up on the ship? I wouldn't have to deal with him, I wouldn't have to see him night after night across the base campfire. I'm going to have to put every bit of myself into the scientific aspects of this expedition, Len; I can't have my mind complicated by the presence of a Vulcan. I can't be torn apart that way."

"Then we really are in a pickle. Between my professionalism, and my emotions, and *your* professionalism, and *your* emotions, we are going to have such a hodgepodge going down on Arachnae that I don't see how we're going to accomplish *anything*."

McCoy reached up to stroke her hair. "The most I can promise is to do my best to make sure Spock stays out of the way. I'll assign Rigel to him, and I'll serve as an intermediary. We'll get it done, and we'll do our jobs the best we can. There's nothing else that Star Fleet can ask of us."

Even as he spoke, though, McCoy knew he was lying. Star Fleet was capable of demanding *everything* from them on Arachnae—including their lives.

9

We are now in orbit around the planet Arachnae, and the situation aboard the *Enterprise,* while tense, is not nearly as difficult as I had assumed it would be. My only problem is making it quite clear to Dr. Tremain that she and Spock are coleaders of the expedition to the planet's surface. According to Dr. McCoy, Tremain still insists that she could carry out the expedition on her own with a picked team of technicians, while Mr. Spock remains aboard ship to coordinate. This plan is totally unacceptable to both myself and Mr. Spock. It will become necessary for me to speak to Dr. Tremain before she and Mr. Spock leave for the planet's surface. I am not pleased that such a conversation is necessary.

Captain Kirk had had very little time to devote to the problems of Katalya Tremain. In the interval between leaving Starbase Eleven and reaching Arachnae, he had been in constant contact with the Federation Council. Opinions were still divided on how to handle the Romulan situation, and Kirk had been given orders that he was not to engage in open warfare with any Romulan vessels he might find in the area. The question had come up as to exactly when Arachnae would belong to the Romulans—when it entered the Neutral Zone, when its system entered Romulan space, or when the planet itself crossed the border into the Romulan Empire. Captain Kirk followed the various arguments by subspace radio with great interest. However, they had very little practical application to the problem at hand. The ion storm that was warping the boundary of the Neutral Zone was accelerating faster and faster across the fabric of space. By the time the *Enterprise* reached Arachnae, the Neutral Zone had swallowed up the orbits of the two outermost planets of the system; it would be only a matter of hours before Arachnae itself was into the Neutral Zone. There had been as yet no sign of a Romulan vessel, but Kirk knew that when Arachnae was finally in the Neutral Zone, the Romulans would be there.

Pressure on board the ship increased as the expedition was readied to go to the surface. Speed was essential. The decision to have a base camp had been reached long before the *Enterprise* came to Arachnae; now Kirk was debating the wisdom of such a decision.

Should the Romulans arrive in orbit around Arachnae while the expedition was down on the planet, it would be very difficult to beam up personnel from the surface. If, however, there was no camp, there would be no base for defense against the Romulans on the surface. Kirk carefully weighed the pros and cons of the situation, and in the quiet of the early morning hours came to the conclusion that there had to be a base camp.

He realized full well that he might be sending members of his crew into danger, but he had his orders from the Federation: the people of Arachnae must be given a choice. Kirk tried not to think about the possibility of having the people under his command die for the freedom of strangers; but he realized as he tossed back and forth on his bed that when he had become captain of the *Enterprise,* he had taken on himself, not only the glory of being a starship captain, but the burdens as well. The decisions of life or death were his. He could, at the last moment, decide not to send Spock to the surface; that way, should there be trouble, his First Officer would be safe and Dr. Tremain would be left on the surface of Arachnae to face the difficulties by herself.

Kirk admitted to himself that his feelings toward Dr. Tremain were a mixture of antipathy for her beliefs and a nagging curiosity as to what she was like as a person. He knew that McCoy was fast falling in love with the woman, and the idea did not distress him. But the possibility that that love might lead to Katalya Tremain becoming a permanent part of the *Enterprise* was not one that Kirk could face with any degree of calm. He simply did not want the woman on board any longer than was necessary. He realized that, should she die on Arachnae, it would be very painful for McCoy—but it would solve the problem nicely.

He had kept the ship in orbit for six hours, using the final checking of the base camp equipment as an excuse. In reality, he was trying to prepare himself for the talk he knew he must have with Katalya Tremain —a talk he did not look forward to. He also needed time to think about the myriad possibilities that might arise from the Arachnae problem. Now his decisions were made: there would be a base camp, and both Tremain and Spock would be assigned to it. There was nothing left to consider. The talk he had to have with Tremain had been worked out in his mind; all the points he had to cover were properly arranged. There was nothing he could do but sleep for a few hours, until he could confront Tremain. Kirk rolled over on his side and pulled the bed-covering tighter around his shoulders. He had a long time ago taught himself how to fall asleep almost instantly. It was a necessary skill for a starship captain.

But tonight, for one of the few times in his life, he found it failing him.

Captain Kirk had left a message that Katalya Tremain was to come to his cabin after breakfast. He knew that gave him approximately two hours before the expedition was scheduled to leave for the planet

Arachnae. He felt that would be an adequate amount of time for him to say what he had to say to her, and resolve some of his own doubts.

He'd gotten very little sleep, and was feeling extremely seedy. He'd eaten a light meal, changed into a clean uniform, and had even, in a strangely compulsive burst of energy, tidied his cabin. He was rearranging books and the large pre-Columbian statue on the shelf for the third time when he heard the door-chime indicating that Katalya Tremain was there. He put the statue carefully back in place and turned to face the door. "Come," he called.

The door slid open and revealed Katalya Tremain wearing desert survival gear. The light blue windbreaker bulged around the waist from the various pieces of equipment she had stuffed into the kangaroo pocket. The blue whipcord trousers fit her legs to perfection, and her knee-high black boots gleamed. She was ready for Arachnae. Whether she was ready for Captain Kirk was another matter entirely.

"I thought we ought to have a talk, Dr. Tremain, before you go down to the planet's surface. I haven't had very much time for you over the last few days; as you well know, I've had to keep track of the Council and their decisions concerning Arachnae." His opening speech came out in a burst of words. He felt he had to say something, and perhaps reminding her of his own importance on this expedition might help to put her in the proper frame of mind for what he had to tell her.

Tremain walked across the room and stood at relaxed attention in front of him. Her eyes were wary, her face set with a look of cold determination. "I've been told the Vulcan *is* going to the planet's surface. I'm very disappointed to have my opinions and scientific judgment set aside so easily," she said.

"The idea that Spock might remain behind never occurred to anyone but yourself. It was never under consideration at any time, and you knew that." It would have been so easy to agree with this woman, to say, "You're right, Doctor, Spock does not belong down on the surface, he could do a better job coordinating up here." But Kirk knew it would have been a less than proper decision and it would not have been in the best interests of the expedition. Spock was needed on Arachnae.

"I didn't ask you here, Doctor, to discuss at this last minute whether Spock would be going to the surface—that's settled. Rather, there are several questions I had to ask you about your own involvement in this expedition." Kirk was unsure how to voice his own paranoia, but it was a subject that had to be brought up, if only for his own peace of mind. Of course, he knew full well that even if she were an agent, she would not be likely to blurt it out just because he asked. But Kirk was sure he could tell, from the twitches of facial muscles, from the reaction in her eyes, and from exactly what she said in response, whether she was telling the truth or not. "I have this paranoid itch, you see. I've been wondering for some time about the possibility that you're here to sabotage this mission."

Tremain's eyebrows lifted and her mouth opened in surprise. "You've *got* to be kidding! I am a scientist, Captain, not a spy. If you think I'm a Romulan, have me sent back down to McCoy and checked out again with another physical. You'll find there's been no surgery done on *my* ears. I'm here for one purpose only: to present an expert opinion on the intelligence of the beings on Arachnae—no more, no less."

Kirk was reassured by her startled indignation at his question; it went far to convince him of her innocence. "I'm sorry to have upset you. But you see, the situation in the Council is still mixed concerning Arachnae. Sarek, as you probably know, has been doing a great deal to split the Council on the question."

"Yes, I had heard the Vulcan was doing some sort of self-serving blather about Arachnae. I believe his opinion was that, even should they prove intelligent, there would be no need to go to the rescue of the Arachnians. It's the sort of treacherous suggestion I would expect of someone like Sarek."

"Well, it seems he's modified his opinion somewhat," Kirk said. "Now he is stating that he's quite convinced that they are *not* intelligent. He has been studying a lot of the reports from previous expeditions —the same ones, I might point out, that you and Spock have been privy to."

"How like a Vulcan. He probably changed his opinion to something more suitable to the minds of most of the Council members; saying that they're animals will probably get him off the hook somewhat. I'd compliment him—even though I don't like him very much."

"Actually, I don't think I've ever met the Vulcan who was willing to change his opinion because it wasn't popular." Kirk's words were coolly weighed out and measured. "I doubt he changed his opinions for that purpose. Do you know Ambassador Sarek, Dr. Tremain? I do. And a more stubborn, opinionated man I've never met in my life. He does have a thoroughgoing belief in his own rightness—and I've seen him use that against his own son. But none of this changes my basic belief in that man's integrity. In fact, I am more inclined to agree with your opinion that the Arachnians are animals, simply because Sarek has come to the same conclusion."

Tremain laughed and relaxed a little more. "Captain, do you mind if I sit down? Talking about Vulcans standing up is a bit wearying." Kirk smiled and quickly pulled up a chair for her, gesturing her to sit down. He sat down at his desk, across from her, his elbows resting on the shiny surface with his chin cradled lightly in his interlaced fingers.

"I think, Captain, you're trying to be deliberately provocative by bringing up the question of Sarek of Vulcan. No, I've never met him. I don't want to. I have no particular interest in meeting any Vulcan. But you're using the same technique that your First Officer used—that of trying to change my mind simply by pointing out that a Vulcan agrees with me. That's neither here nor there. As you yourself said, we both had access to the same records." She smiled slightly, remembering her encounter with Spock. "Besides, Captain, Mr. Spock disagrees with me. It appears I have one Vulcan for and one against—and the opinions of both of them mean nothing to me. Now, don't you think we ought to begin discussing something of some relevance—such as who is in charge on the surface of Arachnae?"

"You and Spock will share joint responsibility," Kirk said. "Spock will be in charge primarily of the establishment of the base camp, and you will be devoting most of your attention to a study of the Arachnians themselves. Spock, however, will back you up on that study. I want both opinions; and needless to say, so does Star Fleet. Dr. McCoy will handle all medical sections, and Lieutenant Rigel will be in charge of any specimens to be captured. Are there any other questions?"

"Captain, I protest being made co-commander with Mr. Spock. I understand full well that I have to go down to the surface with him; I don't like it, but I accept that. But I will not accept the sharing of authority. I was given to understand that I would be in charge of this expedition. I don't like the way I'm being treated, and I will protest to Star Fleet when this expedition is over." Katalya Tremain was furious. Her face had taken on a deep pink cast. Her mouth was set in a tight, narrow line.

"I'm getting very tired of hearing what you like or do not like, or want or do not want. This is a military situation, with orders laid down by Star Fleet, and you will have to obey. You and Spock will be co-commanders of the expedition. Do you understand me?"

Tremain leaned back in her chair and took a deep breath. She slowly relaxed, the pink coloration fading from her cheeks. "It appears, Captain, that I don't have very much choice. I simply have to accept whatever you or, as you claim, Star Fleet, have decided for the expedition. I only hope that I will be able to get my work done and achieve something of some value on Arachnae. You asked me when I first came in here whether I was sent to sabotage the expedition. I assured you I was not. Everyone around me, however, seems so determined to make my job as unpleasant as possible that I'm beginning to wonder whether I'm the only loyal member of Star Fleet on the ship. You have no idea how difficult this is going to be for me. Everything Commodore Stone told me about the expedition is proving to be incorrect. I'm not in charge of it, I'm being hampered by a Vulcan, and you have been decidedly rude. You've not listened to my side of this question at all; you've been unwilling to see any opinion save that of your First Officer. And, Captain, I do object. If anything goes wrong on Arachnae, I refuse to be held responsible for it."

Captain Kirk found himself disturbed by Tremain's accusations. He quickly reviewed in his own mind his treatment of her. Had he been unfair? Unjust? He admitted to himself that he was functioning from a very pro-Vulcan standpoint, but Dr. McCoy had stated that he had not been able to find the root cause for Tremain's behavior, and her constant refusal to be Sigmunded again did make it difficult to look on her views with any sort of favor.

"I'm sorry if I seem harsh," he said. He wanted to make some kind of conciliatory gesture, but he was unsure how she would take it. He admitted to himself that he had made no effort to get to know her —and had, in fact, very eagerly consigned her to the ranks of the expendable. It was a position James Kirk did not like finding himself in. He had been unchivalrous.

He reached one hand out across the table. Tremain looked at him for a moment, then reached out her own hand until their fingers touched. "I have been more than a little distant toward you," Kirk continued. "This mission is important to Star Fleet, and perhaps the situation on Arachnae will be very difficult for you. I can only ask that you try to handle it with as much grace as you can. I admit I took Spock's side in deciding that he was to be co-commander on the expedition, but I felt this was so important to us and the Federation that it will take two people to handle all the details. Please try to understand, even if we don't agree on what I had to do."

Her fingers moved slowly down his palm until the two of them were clasping hands. There was a warmth that Kirk could sense in her, a large segment of herself that she had never shown him before. He began to have some small inkling of what Dr. McCoy saw in Katalya Tremain.

"It's all right, Captain. I'll do my job, and Mr. Spock will no doubt do his, and we'll try not to be at each other's throats. I know I've lost, and I'll try to do it with—what was your word?—'grace.' Yes, I do think I can manage that. But, oh Lord, it will not be easy."

Kirk let go of her hand and stood up. "Would you care for a cup of tea, Doctor?" he asked pleasantly. When she nodded acceptance, he moved over to the food selector and punched out a pot of tea and assorted accouterments to go with it. When the food-delivery door opened, he carried the loaded tray back to the table and for a few moments they were engrossed in the mundane ritual of tea-pouring, sugar and cream, and checking out the assortment of small cookies and cakes that the computer had selected for them.

The atmosphere in the room was much more relaxed. Kirk was grateful for it. He disliked very much the idea that he might be sending this woman to her death simply because he did not understand her.

"I asked Mr. Spock to join us here as soon as he made sure that everything was ready for the base camp. I want to give the two of you together your final instructions on the Arachnae situation."

Tremain stared down into the swirling amber fluid in her teacup. "Yes, I suppose that is necessary. We'll need to know what the *Enterprise*'s position is should the Romulans appear. It's something that makes me very nervous." She looked up at Kirk. "I'm afraid of dying down there, Captain. I'm afraid that you have already decided that the base camp is expendable. And to die by the hands of the Romulans horrifies me."

"It horrifies me, too; I don't intend to let anyone in my command die on Arachnae." Kirk was unwilling to admit that Katalya Tremain's opinion of her expendability was correct. He smiled at her, using his relaxed-seductive smile. "I do want you to come back from this expedition, Dr. Tremain. Of course, I want everyone to come back—but in your case, I think I've neglected my duty in not getting to know you better." The smile deepened into seduction stage II. "In fact, I wish we had more time before you went down to Arachnae—I might get to know you very well."

Tremain lifted one eyebrow in a very Spocklike gesture. "Well, well, Captain. Are you wanting to add me to your collection? You may not realize it, but your reputation with ladies has become legendary. I assure you, I don't need to learn how to kiss; I found that out a long time ago."

Kirk felt as though someone had suddenly drenched him with a large bucket of icewater. Any tenuous feelings of warmth were very rapidly disappearing. He found that he really didn't like Katalya Tremain very much.

Kirk was saved from the embarrassment of making an angry retort by the sound of the doorchime, the door opening, and Spock walking into the room. Kirk found himself very pleased at the presence of his First Officer; it extricated him from a sticky situation with only slight loss of face.

"Well, Spock, would you care to join us for some tea?" Kirk said with false heartiness. "I'll get another cup."

"That won't be necessary, Captain. I have just finished my own breakfast and feel no need of anything more. But I will join you at the table." Spock slid his angular body into one of the curved white chairs. He placed his elbows on the table and pyramided his fingertips. Peering over the top of the self-constructed arch, he looked first at his captain and then at Dr. Tremain. When Tremain looked down and busied herself with chasing two or three cookie crumbs across her plate, Spock looked away from her and faced his captain again.

"Everything is prepared for the base camp, sir. In fact, Mr. Scott is ready to beam the equipment down. I have requested two security guards. I think that should be adequate, since there are only four of the scientific team going down, including Dr. Tremain and myself."

"Four?" Tremain exclaimed. "But I ordered at least eight scientists and six security guards. What do you mean by changing that? Don't I have some say about who will be accompanying us?"

"I felt your request to be unnecessarily broad-based. There was a duplication of effort that was unnecessary. I reviewed the personnel roster, and came to the conclusion that besides the two of us, only Mendoza and McCoy would be necessary. The others were superfluous." Spock's voice was calm, even, and left no room for argument.

Tremain, however, was prepared to argue. "But we don't know what conditions will be like down there. We don't know how dangerous these creatures are. The reports of past expeditions have been sketchy about their fighting ability. I wanted to be sure that there *was* duplication." Tremain was banging her fist against the tabletop in rhythm with her words. "We need backups. Have you taken into consideration what would happen if the Romulans should arilve? We may be cut off from the ship. You are simply not thinking, Mr. Spock."

"I assure you, Dr. Tremain, I always *think*." Spock leaned back in his chair, relaxed and at ease—a complete opposite to Dr. Tremain, who was very quickly becoming livid with anger.

She rose from her chair and began to pace the room. "I won't have it. I won't have it! I have been very obliging about all of this, I have allowed you, Captain Kirk, to talk me into giving up the command of this expedition, I have allowed the presence of that ... Vulcan on the planet's surface, I have been very, very good about giving way when I was asked politely. But I utterly refuse to go any further. We need the extra personnel."

Kirk realized that it would be necessary for him to end the argument. He found himself inclined to agree with Tremain. She *had* been obliging, though not always gracefully, and it did not seem to Kirk to be a very important point to argue about. If she felt a larger crew was necessary, it was a small concession for Spock to make.

"Spock, I think this is one that you're not going to win. Dr. Tremain is entitled to backups. Please order four more guards and the other technical staff people to report to the Transporter Room."

Spock nodded assent, got up from the table and walked over to Captain Kirk's communications console. He quickly placed the order for the four extra guards and added the names of Rigel, Ackroyd, Martin, and Jeffreys to the beam-down list. He closed the channel and turned to face the still-fuming Dr. Tremain.

"According to the most recent study of the ion storm, Doctor," he said, "the magnetic field that defines the Neutral Zone is within six million, three hundred and eighteen thousand, two hundred and seven kilometers. At its present rate of expansion it can be expected to engulf the orbit of Arachnae within thirty-six point one eight hours. It was my opinion that, with the possibility of Romulans presenting themselves the moment the Neutral Zone engulfs Arachnae, it would have been to our best advantage to have as few people on the planet as possible. I would prefer being sure of beaming the entire party up in one trip. Does that change your opinion at all?"

"You have got to be kidding!" Tremain's face was a study in horror. "We have only thirty-six hours before the Romulans are likely to show up? It isn't possible for us to do the work that Star Fleet expects of us in that short a time. They're sending us on a suicide mission. Captain," she turned to face Kirk, "I really must protest. I know I've done a great deal of that in the past hour, but you must admit that the situation is ridiculous."

Kirk sat slumped in his chair, unsure of just what to say next. The sudden vision of Spock and everyone in the landing party being killed by Romulans was entirely too clear to him. He too realized that he would have to protest. Star Fleet could not mean to allow the sacrifice of its personnel for no purpose whatsoever. "You're right, Dr. Tremain. Thirty-six hours is not enough time. Mr. Spock, I suggest you contact Star Fleet and get an opinion. Give them all the pertinent data. And—we wait."

"I'm sorry, Captain," Spock said, "but the wait will not be necessary. I took it upon myself to contact Star Fleet eight hours ago, as soon as I had finished reading the last report on the movement of the Neutral Zone. Star Fleet informed me that we were to go ahead with the mission. In their opinion, the presence of Fleet personnel on the surface of Arachnae might slow down a Romulan takeover."

"Marvelous. Just simply marvelous. Even Star Fleet thinks we're expendable," Tremain said. "What do those bloody-minded fools think they're doing? Captain, are you going to allow this?"

"It doesn't appear I have much choice. Spock, did you attempt to reason with them?"

"They were not in a very reasonable state of mind, Captain. And since it does take the better part of two hours for a message to reach Star Fleet from this quadrant, I felt further discussion would be a waste of energy. We have our orders. Our next step, it seems, is beaming down to Arachnae."

Tremain glared at the Vulcan. "How like a member of your race. You simply accept Star Fleet's orders blindly. Are you that willing to die, Vulcan? I'm not."

Spock flexed his hands and looked down at them as though seeing them for the first time. "No, I am not that eager to die. But I am willing to follow Star Fleet's orders. I feel that you are overestimating our danger. It appears to me that the proper course of action is to beam down to Arachnae, do what we can in the time allotted, and return to the *Enterprise*. In that way we will have performed our job according to Star Fleet specifications—and, I might add, we will not be eligible for court-martial. Don't you agree, Captain?"

Kirk was caught in a trap of Star Fleet's making. He could send down a party of technicians to the planet's surface and keep Spock, Tremain, McCoy, and Rigel aboard ship; but that was not what Star Fleet had had in mind. His paranoid itch was back, and this time it wasn't directed at Tremain. Someone out there in Star Fleet, the Federation, or the great Universe itself, was trying to make life extremely difficult for James T. Kirk.

Mr. Scott stood behind the transporter console, looking very grim. He had beamed down the six security guards, Mendoza, Martin, Jeffreys, Ackroyd, and the equipment for the base camp half an hour ago, and all reports from the planet's surface indicated that events were proceeding as planned. There was no sign of the Arachnians—nor of the Romulans. But Scotty was still uneasy. He was not looking forward to beaming down the rest of the party. He was as unsure as Tremain of the dangers of this expedition, and he felt somehow like a murderer. The door to the Transporter Room opened, and Captain Kirk, Mr. Spock, and Dr. Tremain entered.

"Are you ready to beam us down, Mr. Scott?" Spock inquired.

"Aye, sir, for all the good it'll do you. I must say, Captain, that I don't approve of this at all. But I don't suppose Star Fleet would be asking an engineer's permission to commit murder."

"Belay that, Mr. Scott." Kirk's voice was firm. He was trying hard not to agree with Scotty. He had years of Star Fleet training to stiffen his spine, but he didn't like the situation any more than his chief engineer did. Kirk looked around the Transporter Room. "Where are Dr. McCoy and Lieutenant Rigel? I was told they would be meeting us here. See if you can find them, Scotty. It's important that we get the rest of the party down to the surface as quickly as possible. They've got just a little over thirty-five hours."

"Aye, sir. Dr. McCoy and Lieutenant Rigel said they would be here as soon as they could—I'm surprised at the delay. But I'll contact Sick Bay again." Scotty turned to the wall communications grill and was connected, not to McCoy's office, but to Lieutenant Rigel's lab. He was somewhat surprised at this and turned to tell his captain so, but before he could open his mouth, sounds of a struggle and an ungodly scream came from the speaker. Kirk sprinted toward the grill and yelled into it, "Bones! Bones, are you all right? What was that scream?"

"It was that blasted, blathering idiot of a mongcat," the doctor's voice said. "Lieutenant Rigel's pet. It doesn't want her to leave and now she's chasing it all over the lab. We'll be there as soon as we possibly can, Jim."

Kirk leaned his forehead against the smooth metal panel and wondered what he'd done to get the Universe this upset at him. He quietly wished that he had become a farmer instead of a Star Fleet officer. "Take care of it *now*, Bones, and get down here. I want to get this farce over with. Kirk out."

He slammed his fist against the off button, taking a certain savage satisfaction in how much it hurt his hand. He slowly turned around and faced Tremain and Spock. "Well, I would suggest that you two go ahead and beam down to the surface. From what I know of Rigel's Fuzzybutt, it's going to take them a good hour to get that thing caught. I wish I hadn't allowed pets on the *Enterprise*. First tribbles, now mongcats. . . ."

Tremain went up to the transporter chamber, taking her position on one of the disks. "Are you coming, Mr. Spock?" she asked.

Spock nodded assent, walked to the platform and took his position on a disk near Tremain. "Beam us down, Mr. Scott," he said, in a voice slightly tinged with annoyance.

Tremain was about to remark on this slight show of emotion when the transporter effect cut her off and, in twin columns of shimmering light, Katalya Tremain and Mr. Spock vanished from the *Enterprise*.

10

Arachnae hung in space like a red and blue cabochon. Its seas were shallow, its land masses large, its atmosphere thin and dry. The equatorial band had been found to be totally uninhabitable. The coordinates fed into the computer for the beam-down point had been set for one of the large continents in the northern hemisphere.

The transporter deposited Spock and Tremain on a ledge overlooking the site of the base camp. The view from the ledge was impressive. Mountains composed of slabs of red rock reached toward the sky. Canyons cut deep by rushing water appeared to be bottomless. There was a river at the base of the hill, one of the reasons why this site had been chosen, running blood-red with suspended silt. There was some ground cover, small stunted trees, scrub and hardy desert grasses, and overhead the sky was clear turquoise blue with thin streaks of cloud.

"Shall we join the rest of the crew, Dr. Tremain?" Spock said. Without waiting for an answer, he began making his way down a narrow path to the floor of the small notch between two sloping hills. Tremain followed slowly behind.

The camp had been well arranged by the base team. Lieutenant Angela Mendoza had put herself in charge of getting all inflatable shelters properly circled around the firepit. The security guards had as-

wounds were unpleasant, he was not in as much danger as Mendoza. Taking out his communicator, he flipped it open and requested an *Enterprise* channel. "Captain?" he said in a deceptively even voice. "I would advise that you beam us out of here immediately. We have two severely injured crewpeople, a number of men dead, and I would not care to wager anything on the possibility of the Arachnians staying out of the area very much longer. We are in danger here."

There was a long silence from the communicator, and then Kirk's voice. "We can't beam you up, Spock. We have a problem of our own. The Romulans have arrived."

11

Captain's Log, Stardate 6459.6:

An unexpected anomaly in the ion storms has
caused further complications to our mission. By moving
the border of the Neutral Zone faster than anticipated,
the planet Arachnae has entered the Zone earlier
than our estimates had predicted. Along with the
Neutral Zone came a Romulan cruiser. Technically, it
has no right to be in the Neutral Zone—but neither
for me to beam up the landing party.
do we. I have put up my shields in case the Romulans
should attack—but that now makes it impossible

Kirk sat in his command chair on the Bridge and
pounded his fist into the armrest in sheer frustration
as he listened to Spock's report of the damage on the
planet below. Five security guards and three members
of the technical party were dead; a crewwoman was
dying of severe shock and blood loss, a man was
wounded—and there was nothing whatsoever that
Kirk could do about it.

He looked up at the viewscreen in front of him.
It was filled by the image of a falcon ship—a
Romulan vessel. "Lieutenant Uhura, open a channel to
the Romulan cruiser. We've got to make arrangements
to beam Spock, Tremain, and those two crewmembers
up."

Lieutenant Uhura looked up from her communication board, a startled expression on her normally impassive face. "But Captain, we don't dare let down the shields. The Romulans won't allow anyone to beam to or from the ship. They're sure to fire on us."

"I know only too well what the Romulans are like, Lieutenant, but this involves beaming up injured personnel. They do have some sense of decency. Now open that channel at once!"

Lieutenant Uhura turned back to her communication board and sent the signal to the Romulan ship. The image on the viewscreen shifted to one of the interior of the Romulan vessel, where a figure stood proudly on the bridge—an elderly, frustrated eagle of a man. The Romulan Commander faced Kirk, waiting.

"Commander, this is James Kirk of the *Enterprise*. I request permission to beam up four members of my crew from the planet's surface," Kirk said, knowing full well that the odds were against his receiving such permission.

"Captain Kirk, I am Maximinus Thrax, commander of the *Decius,* and I have no interest in the requests of a treaty breaker like yourself. This planet is now in the Neutral Zone, and neither of us has any right to place troops on it. If you do have people there, they are there illegally, and are no concern of mine."

The acceleration change of the Neutral Zone boundary had caught everyone by surprise, enveloping Arachnae before the *Enterprise* could warn its party on the ground. Kirk had tried desperately to reach the base camp party, but had gotten no answer until the communication from Spock. He had, of course, put his shields up immediately at the first sign of the Romulan ship, and then Spock had called, putting an even more horrible pressure on the situation.

Kirk quickly sized Thrax up as a blustering tyrant of a man, unlikely to be at all reasonable. The

Romulan Commander's answer was only proving that assessment correct.

"I do not believe you have anyone on the planet's surface," the Romulan continued. "I think this is some sort of underhanded Federation trick. We know you very well from past encounters, James Kirk, and we know that you are totally untrustworthy." Thrax turned to someone offscreen and said something in a language that was unintelligible to Kirk. The viewscreen went black.

Kirk leaned back in his command chair and glowered at the empty screen. He slammed his fist down hard on one of the communications buttons. "Dr. McCoy, report to the Bridge," he snarled.

Kirk was not angry at McCoy, but rather at the Universe itself. McCoy, though, was closer at hand. Kirk sat drumming his fingers on the arm of his chair until the doctor arrived on the Bridge. "Bones, you've got to do something, give them some advice at least down on the surface. Angela Mendoza is dying down there."

McCoy approached the command chair and placed his hands on the back of it. Kirk could tell from the expression on his face that there was more bad news to come.

"She's dead, Jim. While you were talking to the Romulan, Spock sent up another call. Angela Mendoza bled to death while he and Tremain were searching through the wreckage to try and put together enough of a first-aid kit to help her. I'm sorry."

Kirk closed his eyes for a moment and took a deep breath. He opened his eyes again, his face deceptively calm. "Lieutenant Uhura, turn on the automatic signal to let Spock knew he must maintain radio silence; if he broadcasts too much more, the Romulans may be able to zero in on his location. Then open another channel to the Romulan ship."

Kirk waited until the screen again showed the image of the Romulan Commander. "Commander

Thrax, one of my crew members just died on the planet's surface because of your refusal to let us beam her up. I hold you responsible—and you *will* pay for it."

On board the *Decius,* Commander Maximinus Thrax drew himself to his full height facing the viewscreen and the Federation Captain shown upon it. "Captain, I deny all responsibility for you or your ship—and if the *Enterprise* does not leave the vicinity of Arachnae the moment the Romulan boundary reaches it, we will blast you out of the sky. Commander Maximinus Thrax out." He abruptly shut down the two-way communication. The moment the screen was safely black, Thrax grabbed the edge of the communications panel and sagged. A young man moved swiftly to his side, caught him, and eased him downward into a chair.

"Father, you're taking this too hard," the young man said. "You can win this, you know. Arachnae is ours as soon as the Neutral Zone passes completely by it. The Captain of the *Enterprise* will have no right to stop us."

"Licinius, we know full well that this man James Kirk is not inclined to be reasonable. Look what he's done to every other Romulan commander who's gone up against him. Oh, I wish I were back home. I wish I were tending my garden. I'm too old for this sort of thing. And if I fail, I will be disgraced."

"But sir, we are already in disgrace. I suspect Proconsul Servius Tullis ordered us here because I refused to marry his daughter. He wants us to die at the hands of the Federation." The young man reached out to clasp his father's shoulder. His was a beautifully intelligent face, enough like Spock's to seem like a younger relative. He was slender, fine-boned, and hopeful.

"Then the Proconsul will succeed. We know this

man Kirk. He'll kill us all if we do not destroy ourselves. We have no chance." Thrax buried his face in
his hands. "We're doomed, all of us," he moaned.

"Are you really going to let the Proconsul win
that easily, Father? It's not your fault you're here, it's
mine. You should have been allowed to spend the
rest of your life in quiet retirement. But I can't take
command for you. You have to solve this problem."
The young man paused for a moment, aware that he
was about to say something that would be very painful for his father, but nonetheless the truth. "I mean
no disrespect, but you should have allowed the Federation Captain to beam up his landing party. He
sounded as though he would not easily forgive the
death of a crewmember."

"I was afraid it was a trap. I was so sure that if
I said yes, Kirk would see it as a sign of weakness.
No matter what happens, we cannot let this man
know that we are weaker than he is. Llciniuo, if he
had any such suspicions, he would fall on us like a
ravening wolf."

"I ask your pardon for what I am about to say,
but say it I must. You are in error, my father. By
attempting to do nothing wrong, you are doing nothing right." The young man sank to his knees beside
his father's chair. "Renounce me for an unfilial son,
but I must tell you that which is true."

Maximinus Thrax lifted his head and straightened
his back, and for a moment the ghost of the commander he had once been appeared in his eyes. He
turned and looked down at his son. "Stand up," he
said sternly. "A son of my house should bow to no
man, not even his father. I will deal with Kirk in a
way befitting a Romulan. I regret the death of his
crewwoman, and I regret my own inaction. It will not
happen again, my son."

On the planet's surface, Dr. Tremain looked down
at the dead body of Angela Mendoza lying on the
ground. The woman's dark hair was matted with

blood, her uniform sodden with it. There was nothing further that Tremain could do. She got slowly to her feet and looked out over the ravaged camp. The weary lines in her face betrayed the pain and anguish she felt. Tremain tried hard not to think of Mendoza's last few minutes—the painful and hurried search through the wreckage for something to stop the bleeding. It had been a race against time, and they had lost.

She turned away from the body to watch Spock clumsily attempting to bandage the security guard's wounds. How long, she wondered, would Williams live?

"What are his chances, Mr. Spock?" she asked aloud. There was no hostility in her voice; she was too tired, and there was just no time for any emotion.

"Acceptable. I have done what I could, but I am not a doctor. I hesitate to admit it, but I would greatly welcome McCoy's company at this time." Spock leaned back on his heels and reexamined the bandages. "This will hold him for a while. But if he does not receive special care. . . ." He shrugged. "I would recommend that he be beamed up to the ship as soon as possible."

"And if pigs had wings, they'd roost in trees. Williams is just going to have to make do with you and me, Mr. Spock, because the chances of getting him up to the *Enterprise* appear very slim at the moment. I just tried to reach the ship again, and got the recorded message ordering us to maintain radio silence."

She changed the subject abruptly. "Did Williams manage to tell you anything about what happened? Did he explain?" Tremain knelt in the dust beside the now only semiconscious lieutenant. She reached out and placed her hand palm down across his forehead. "I think he's getting a fever," she said.

"I was afraid of something of that nature," Spock said. "But I could not ascertain it as easily as you might. My body temperature is such that even should a human be in the midst of a raging fever, he would feel chill to me. But as to your question, Williams managed to tell me very little—only that they were taken by surprise, that it was very sudden and they had little time to defend themselves. They kept their phasers on stun." Spock looked searchingly at Tremain. "Something I observed that you did not do, Doctor. You had your phaser set on kill. Why? Some form of primitive revenge?"

Tremain shook her head. "No, something far more basic. And in fact I'm going to have to kill every Arachnian left alive, stunned, in the camp. You see, Mr. Spock, the stun will wear off in an hour or two—and they will be here, and we will be here. And personally," she glanced around the camp, mentally toting up the number of stunned Arachnians, "I don't like the odds." She got to her feet and drew her phaser.

Spock reached out his hand toward Tremain and then stopped in midgesture. He realized that she was behaving in a perfectly logical manner. The Arachnians in the camp, sentient or not, had to die. It would not be possible for the two of them to manage that many of the beings alone, and it was unlikely that the natives would calmly leave the area when they returned to consciousness. Spock turned away so he would not have to watch Tremain. He busied himself with making Lieutenant Williams as comfortable as possible, covering him with shreds of fabric from the badly damaged tent. He tried not to listen to the sound of phaserfire. But each time Tremain fired, Spock's body jerked almost imperceptibly.

A shout from Tremain pulled Spock swiftly out of introspection. He jumped to his feet and ran toward the woman.

She was standing beside the outcropping of rock beneath which the Arachnians had vanished. There were a number of Arachnian bodies lying around the entrance slab, and those of several other creatures as well. Tremain was kneeling by the side of a large shaggy gray object; she reached out to touch it and drew back her hand swiftly. "What is it, Mr. Spock?

I've never seen anything quite like it. There's at least eight or nine of them all around this outcropping."

Spock knelt beside her while holding out his tricorder, and watched the viewscreen as the facts concerning the creature were registered. "I think I've seen something like this before—on Janus VI, to be precise. They're known as hortas. There's one difference, of course—the ones on Janus VI were an orange color, these are not. I would suggest, Dr. Tremain, that we attempt to spare these creatures. The one that I had contact with on Janus VI was intelligent; these may be also. I cannot precisely guarantee that this is a horta; however, judging by the readings on my tricorder, there is a great deal of similarity."

"Very well, Mr. Spock, I'll accept your authority in this matter. I'll take care of the rest of the Arachnians, and you can see if you can make some sort of contact with the creature." She looked at him for a moment. "You *do* use mindmeld, don't you, Mr. Spock?"

Spock glanced up at her quickly. A look of surprise was on his face. "I did not know you were familiar with the mindmeld," he said. "However, I am reluctant to use the technique on this creature until I have seen some positive signs of its intelligence. Mindmelding with an animal can have serious consequences, such as my taking on that creature's more feral qualities."

"Of course I knew about the mindmeld technique; it's always advisable to know everything possible about one's adversaries." Tremain turned her back to Spock and with quiet, cold efficiency blasted another Arachnian into nothingness. When Tremain next glanced up, she noticed that Mr. Spock was moving rapidly back in the direction of Williams. She followed quickly.

They found the man tearing at his bandages and muttering in a thick, gutteral voice. Tremain checked Williams' forehead and found him excessively feverish. "He's burning up. What do you think it is?"

Spock knelt beside the injured crewman and began examining the bandaged wounds. The flesh was swollen, rapidly turning a deep greenish-purple. "I'm afraid we are involved in a situation I had not expected. It appears that the Arachnian bite is far more dangerous than we had supposed." Spock looked at his tricorder and began examining the wounds. "Alkaloid," he said. "And very toxic. My earlier prognosis was overly optimistic. In my estimation, this man does not have long to live."

Unfortunately, Spock was correct. His use of the term "not long to live," however, was relative. While the actual time-span could not have been more than fifteen minutes, the agony Williams suffered must have made it seem like eternity to him. Both Spock and Tremain were needed to hold the man down as his thrashing became more violent. He screamed aloud, calling out to someone that neither Spock nor Tremain could see. He was obviously hallucinating.

His eyes rolled aimlessly; his tongue protruded and a reddish foam flecked the corners of his lips. His disjointed conversation with whomever he perceived turned into an unceasing, keening wail.

Spock gingerly started to reach for the pressure points on Williams' head to try to ease the pain. Tremain lashed out, slapping at his hands.

"Don't you dare mindmeld with him, Vulcan. You have no idea what's going on in there. I do not want to have two of you like this on my hands. And what if he dies? What if what's going on in his mind is what's killing him? Do you want to risk that?"

Spock, amazed, sat back suddenly on his heels and stared at the biologist. Her striking him had taken him quite by surprise, and her obvious concern was simply one more clue to his computerlike mind. "I had no intention of mindmelding," he said quietly. "I had only intended to attempt to ease his pain. Do you mind, Doctor?"

"If you can do anything for him . . . but I think it may be too late."

Spock reached again for the temporal nerve points, but it was indeed too late. The crewman's body arched convulsively, and fell back upon the ground, dead.

"We had better dig graves for our casualties," Spock said, his voice even as he got to his feet and brushed gravel off his knees.

Tremain held back her tears, and tilted her head to look up at him. "What? Are you getting sentimental, Spock? I didn't know you had it in you."

"Sentimentality, my dear Doctor, has nothing to do with it. I only suspect that the presence of the buried bodies might give the Arachnians pause. They know that intelligent creatures bury their dead, and that since we have done so we must also be intelligent creatures."

"Bravo. I *knew* you'd have a logical reason. But that's assuming that *they* are intelligent—an assumption I'm not totally willing to concede as yet." She paused. "I just wish we could notify the ship, but I suppose the Captain is right about maintaining radio silence, even if we all die down here."

"By maintaining radio silence, the Captain is trying to keep us from dying, at least at the hands of the Romulans," Spock said. "We dare not let them know where we are. The silence is a necessity. I am also sure that Captain Kirk has more than enough to cope with at this point without being informed of yet another death."

He looked down at Williams' body, a rather thoughtful expression on his face. "The mindmelding —your concern has given me somewhat of an idea, Dr. Tremain. A possible way to determine once and for all whether the Arachnians are intelligent. If we could capture one, stun it, and then if I were to meld with its mind, we would have an answer."

"Yes, and it's that you're totally insane," Tremain replied. "If you try anything that stupid, Mr. Spock, I personally will use my phaser on you. And it may not be set on stun. Keep that in mind."

"That sounded distinctly like a threat, Dr. Tremain. What I choose to do with my mind is my concern, not yours. And if I choose to mindmeld with an Arachnian, I'm not sure you could stop me." Spock drew his phaser and began digging a trenchlike mass grave for the dead crewmembers.

"What you do with your mind is indeed up to you," Tremain said. "But how that affects me is *my* concern. If you were to mindmeld with an Arachnian and found it was not intelligent, you yourself said that there's a good chance you would take on its animal characteristics—and then how could I be expected to cope with you? You outweigh me, and you're stronger than I am, and I would probably be forced to kill you. So I would prefer to prevent a great deal of trouble and kill you *before* you mindmeld. Now, isn't that logical?"

Spock turned and lifted Williams' head and shoulders, motioning Tremain to carry the dead man's feet. One by one, they transferred all the bodies into the grave and Spock, again using his phaser, covered them with molten slag. He had said nothing during the process of burial, but now, standing beside the grave, he appeared to have completed his contemplation of her logic.

"Your argument, while having some merit, does not take into account the power of the Vulcan mind. I'm sure *I* would be able to overcome any such difficulty. And as I've said many times, I am convinced that the Arachnians are intelligent so the problem should not arise at all."

"Mr. Spock, you're not even trying to imagine what it would be like to share your mind with that of an animal."

"On Vulcan, an overactive imagination is frowned on. Nevertheless, since you feel so strongly about my mindmelding with a possible animal mentality, I will keep your homicidal tendencies in mind. Though I am not really positive you would be capable of killing me."

"Don't bet on it. If you were running around with a savage Arachnian mind, I would kill you so quick your pointed ears would spin. Survival happens to be one of my favorite traits."

"In that case, Doctor, were I to mindmeld with an Arachnian I would make sure you were not in the general vicinity first."

12

Captain's Log, Stardate 6459.7:

I am in the middle of an extremely difficult situation. My First Officer and Dr. Katalya Tremain are stranded on the surface of Arachnae by the presence of a Romulan warship. I have contacted Star Fleet and I am awaiting further instructions. My previous orders were that I was not, under any circumstances, to fire on a Romulan vessel, which ties my hands considerably. But Star Fleet is hours away by subspace communicators, and I know only that I must remain in the area until the Neutral Zone completely passes by the planet and Arachnae is in Romulan space.

The Romulan Commander worries me. He is very obviously a seasoned warrior, and I fear that I may have been sent an adversary whose abilities in battle may exceed my own.

Dr. McCoy had remained on the Bridge, busily weaving himself a garment of guilt. He was sure that terrible things were taking place on the surface of Arachnae, and that he should have been there with Spock and Tremain. Had he not stopped to assist Lieutenant Rigel in catching Fuzzybutt, he might have been able to save Angela Mendoza's life. And the last report from Tremain indicated that Lieutenant Williams was in serious condition. There was nothing

McCoy could do, though, except pace in a narrow circle near the Captain's chair and inflict on himself all the tortures his overly active mind could produce.

It was a time of waiting for everyone aboard the *Enterprise*. Kirk sat in his command chair like a granite statue of some ancient Egyptian god; only his eyes moved from the viewscreen downward to the red alert button and then back again to the viewscreen. Sulu and Chekov were bent over their respective instrument panels, industriously checking and rechecking every bit of data concerning Arachnae, the Neutral Zone, and the Romulan ship which hung silently before them. Lieutenant Uhura sat at her station, earplug in place, waiting tensely for any communication at all.

The elevator door to the turbolift opened and Lieutenant Commander Scott entered the Bridge. "Captain, will you be firing on the Romulan ship? We canna leave Dr. Tremain and Spock on the surface of Arachnae. It'll be getting dark there soon. Considering the problems they've had with the wee beasties, I don't think it'll get any better at night."

"I quite agree with you, Scotty." The statue dissolved and again became Captain Kirk. "But at this moment I have no real justification for firing on the Romulan vessel. My orders from Star Fleet are that I am to 'treat' with the Romulans, to be 'diplomatic,' and under no circumstances to fire at them. The planet *is* going to be theirs in a little while, after all."

Kirk's fist again smashed into the arm of his chair. "Diplomatic! I'm not a diplomat. I'm the captain of a starship. I don't know how to handle this. But handle it I will. Dr. Tremain and Mr. Spock *will* be returned to this ship, and we will avoid a fight with the Romulans. I don't know how, but I am going to pull this off or die trying."

"Jim." McCoy reached out, touched the Captain on the shoulder. "I've got to get down to the planet's surface. It's more than just a matter of Williams. Tremain and Spock shouldn't be alone together down there. It isn't safe—not safe for her, and not safe for him. Why didn't I beam down with them, why did I stop to chase that stupid animal? Ruth could have gotten a tech man to help her. Damnation! I've got to do something to save Katalya."

Kirk turned to face his Medical Officer. "It wasn't your fault, Bones. It was just one of those things. I know you're worried about her, that she means a lot to you, but what you're doing to yourself won't make things any better. I won't beam you down there—it would only complicate matters further. And if you don't stop torturing yourself, I'll give you an order to stop it!" Kirk tried to smile reassuringly. It came out a death's-head grin.

"But I can't help wondering what's going on down there." McCoy resumed walking in a tight little circle. "We haven't heard from them since Mendoza died. What's happening down there?"

Spock leaned back on his heels and reached up to brush his bangs back into place. He looked down at the semiconscious hortalike creature in front of him. "The EEG readings on my tricorder do not indicate a high degree of intelligence. I am quite sure it is a nonsentient animal, and I will not need to mindmeld with it to prove my hypothesis. That would be illogical under the circumstances."

Behind him, Tremain heaved a sigh of relief.

"I do wish I had the equipment for a more detailed study, however," Spock continued. "It is basically of the same family as a horta, and I find that fascinating. It's an indication of some sort of parallel evolution, on planets parsecs apart. This creature secretes a powerful acid that eats through rock at a phenomenal rate—a talent the Arachnians seem to utilize to their own advantage. That is why we were not able to find any indications of Arachnians within a four-kilometer radius, and yet they were upon the camp so rapidly. I wish this creature had been intelligent—it might have answered once and for all the question of the Arachnians' own intelligence. However," he got slowly to his feet, "it might be some indication, considering that the Arachnians obviously have domesticated these creatures, and use them to make their tunnels. That would seem to require intelligence of some sort."

"Not necessarily," Tremain said. "Remember, ants back on Earth herd aphids and utilize them like cows—and I haven't met an intelligent ant yet." She looked down at the shaggy creature and watched it shudder as it came closer to consciousness. "What shall we do with them, Spock? Are they any danger to us?"

"Unlikely. They seem to be rather gentle creatures. I would suspect that if we simply uncovered the opening to the underground passage, they would leave of their own free will. I would regret having to kill them."

"I agree with you. There's been entirely too much killing this afternoon. But I suggest we head back up the hillside to that cave. It would be a lot easier to defend than this open campsite, and perhaps safer. Unless, of course," she looked down at the horta creature which was now awake and groggy, "they use these things to bore right through the mountain to us."

"It is a distinct possibility," Spock admitted. "However, I would prefer not to remain here. I suggest we go through the remains of the camp and salvage as much survival gear as possible. We need food and some form of covering, for it does get cold at night here according to the reports."

The sun was sinking behind the hills by the time Spock and Tremain started for the cave. They had salvaged as much as they could from the destroyed camp, but it added up to a pitiful amount of supplies. There was no food; most of it had been destroyed by the Arachnians or contaminated in the battle. There were only shreds and scraps of the damaged tents to use as covering against the cold. Tremain had managed to find a not too badly dented cooking pot. It was more than she had expected and less than they needed. By the time they reached the mouth of the cave, the sun had vanished altogether, leaving a thin blue twilight.

It was already beginning to get cold. Spock built a fire in the center of the cave floor, utilizing the dried brush from the hillside. Tremain had busied herself gathering armloads of grass to make some pretense of beds. There would be no dinner, unless she could find something on the hillside that might be edible.

"I think I'll try a little hunting close to the mouth of the cave. There's no doubt a number of small nocturnal creatures about. Have you ever tried eating snake, Mr. Spock?"

Spock wondered whether she was attempting to be deliberately provoking. She had told him earlier that she had tried to learn as much about her "adversaries" as possible. He considered a dozen possible comments, and finally thought of an adequate answer. "I do not eat meat, Dr. Tremain. I am by this time, however, acclimatized to the sight of meat being eaten in front of me. If you wish to catch some small creature and eat it, go right ahead. I am perfectly capable of fasting tonight, and when it is daylight I will search for some edible roots or berries."

Tremain nodded and walked out of the cave. Spock could hear her footsteps on the narrow ledge, and then a scrabbling sound as small pebbles bounced down the side of the mountain while she climbed upward. He wondered whether he should have accompanied her—it was getting quite dark, and there was some danger of the Arachnians returning. But he felt that she was intelligent enough to be aware of these facts, and would not go too far from the cave.

Thinking that hot water might be useful to Tremain for her cooking, he busied himself collecting a potful from the trough Tremain had made earlier that day. That time now seemed an incredibly long while ago. Spock balanced the pot carefully over the fire and sat down close to the blaze. There was something oddly comforting about watching the crackling flames.

Tremain returned triumphantly carrying a small rabbitlike creature. She knelt at the lip of the cave and proceeded to expertly skin it and prepare it for cooking. She skewered it on a long twig and propped it over the flames. Spock looked away. The fire was no longer pleasant.

"Oh. I found these." Tremain pulled several small round yellow objects out of the kangaroo pocket of her jacket. "I think they might be edible. But you should doublecheck it with your tricorder first to make sure they aren't toxic to Vulcans." She handed the small squashlike globes to Spock. He analyzed them swiftly and decided they were edible. He tossed them one by one into the pot of boiling water.

"Thank you very much for taking the time to locate those, Dr. Tremain," he said, watching the squashes bounce and toss in the bubbling water. He was, he realized, far more hungry than he would have liked to admit.

Tremain looked down at the rabbit which was beginning to char around the edges. "I would have done the same for anyone. Or for a dog. I never could stand any animal going hungry."

Spock said nothing, but the expression on his face was very thoughtful as he reviewed his accumulation of data on Katalya Tremain and her supposed hatred of Vulcans.

13

On board the *Decius*, Commander Maximinus Thrax and his son had convened a council of war. All the high-ranking officers around the table were either members of the Thrax clan or vassals to it. Proconsul Servius, when he wanted revenge, was very thorough.

"We are facing a situation of grave danger," Licinius said, looking at the men and women gathered around the room. His father had given him the right to lead the meeting. The young man's opportunities for command might be very limited if this particular expedition did not go well. "As you know, we are facing Captain James Kirk of the starship *Enterprise*, a man who in the past we have found to be totally without mercy and thoroughly unscrupulous. We have very little chance of leaving this encounter with honor. But if we die, we die like Romulans. And we will take as many of the Federationists as possible with us. However, it would be preferable if we could achieve our aims without bloodshed. The High Command has been in communication with the Federation Council. That Council is composed solely of timeservers, power-mad conquerors, and men with no moral standards whatsoever. There are, however, a few voices of sanity there, and we can only hope they will prevail. If so, when the Arachnae system is completely within Romulan territory, it is ours. We on this ship must proceed at all times as though the Federation Council will give us our rights. And we must present to the Captain of the *Enterprise* an appearance of being willing to back that opinion with not only our own might, but the might of the entire Romulan Empire—even though we in this room know that this isn't so."

There was a stirring among the officers; conversations begun and cut off; and then silence. Everyone here knew that what Licinius had said was true. The Romulan Empire was not prepared to go to war over the Arachnae system. But it was, in the person of its Proconsul, willing to sacrifice the *Decius* and the Thrax clan. Such political sacrifices were well known in the history of the Empire. Battle was a very convenient way of getting rid of one's enemies. On the massive chessboard of the Universe, the *Decius,* under Commander Thrax, was a pawn that had been sent very deep into the enemy side of the board. And the fact that the dividing line on that board was shifting was of very little importance.

Outside the cave, Spock and Tremain could hear the multitudinous sounds of night. Somewhere off to the west an animal roared; from the sound of its voice, it was probably a carnivore. Closer to the cave, there were scrabbling sounds in the rocks, the minute slitherings of small animals. The river sounded exceedingly loud in the darkness.

Inside the cave, Tremain and Spock huddled a little closer to the fire. They were both too civilized to cope easily with the primitive aspects of the situation in which they found themselves. They had each received months of survival training while at the Academy; but there was still the realization that this was not training—this was reality.

Spock got to his feet and walked slowly to the lip of the cave. He stood peering out into the darkness. "I wish we still had our security alarm system. I would rest a great deal easier tonight with it in place."

"But we don't have it, Mr. Spock, and it did little

good for the camp when we did have it." Tremain had thrown the remaining scraps of meat from her dinner into the fire and was watching them sizzle and burn away into nothing. There was no point in leaving anything that might attract the carnivores to this cave. "It's senseless to wish for what we haven't got. And besides, I think wishing is a very 'illogical' pastime, don't you agree?"

"You're quite right, it is illogical. But nonetheless I would sleep easier. And speaking of sleep, I would suggest we try to get some. We do not have very much time before the Romulans will decide to take this planet. We had best save our strength for any possible confrontation later." Spock came back from the lip of the cave and proceeded to inspect the sleeping arrangements Tremain had set up. They consisted of two piles of grass and leaves, one on each side of the cave as far from each other as possible, together with what shreds of tent fabric and undamaged pieces of thermal blanket Tremain had found. Unfortunately it was most inadequate, considering how rapidly the night air temperature was already dropping. Spock stood looking at one bed and then at the other.

"You are aware," he said, "of the chill already present; I am positive it will get a great deal colder before dawn. I would suggest that your preparations are somewhat inadequate for such cold. Don't you think it would be much more practical if you were to consider sleeping with me?"

"How *dare* you suggest anything of that nature? That is both disgusting and obscene, a betrayal of your commission as an officer and a *gentleman*. I would thank you to keep any such ideas to yourself in the future, Mr. Spock." Tremain got to her feet and stalked to one pile of leaves. "I intend to sleep over here on this side of the cave, and I don't care how cold it gets. I would never consider anything else."

Spock lifted one eyebrow slightly. There was a faint suggestion of a smile at the corners of his mouth.

"I was not suggesting sexual activity, Dr. Tremain," he said with an air of intense innocence. "Although I am aware of the confusion that the phrase 'to sleep with' can lead to. On Vulcan we have no such errors of speech. When we say something, it is precisely what we mean. However, should you wish sexual activity, I'm sure you realize I am fully capable of it at any time I feel sexual desire."

Dr. Tremain stood, fists clenched, slightly crouched, prepared for anything.

"You needn't go into a defensive posture," Spock continued. "My suggestion was meant only as a clarification of my stated offer to conserve our mutual body warmths."

Tremain slowly straightened. A blush stained her cheekbones. "You are impossible, just like most Vulcans I've known. I had not mistaken your suggestion for a proposition, so you can stop being so vile. I knew precisely what you meant. And I don't like the idea of it any more than I like the idea of sex with you. I wouldn't be able to sleep at all in that close a physical contact with a Vulcan."

"Then it might work out for the best. If you were awake all night, you could listen for carnivores and scavengers. In fact, it might be quite efficient."

Spock, or at least some part of his mind, was enjoying the conversation. It was almost as interesting as goading McCoy—in fact, much more interesting.

Across the cave, Katalya Tremain turned and burrowed into the pile of grasses and fabric she had chosen as her bed. She curled up tightly facing the wall, her back to Spock. "Go to bed, Mr. Spock," she said. "And try to be a little less disgusting tomorrow. Or I might be tempted to take a phaser to you—and I might set it on kill!"

Spock climbed into his own improvised bed and arranged it as comfortably around him as he could. He had evolved a plan of action for dealing with Dr. Tremain. Tonight had been only the first step. He had much more in mind for the next day.

What he would have to be very careful of was goading her only enough to get the results he desired. He knew that pushed too far into a corner, she might indeed be capable of killing him.

The morning sunlight was touching the far wall of the cave when Spock awoke. He could see that Tremain had gotten up even earlier. During the night he had heard sounds indicative of how uncomfortable she was finding the cold. He had been tempted to get up and give her some of his own bedcoverings, but he was not sure how she would have taken such a gesture.

He lay curled up in his improvised cocoon, watching Tremain across the cave. She had put a bucket of water on to heat, and was now bathing her hands, face and the upper part of her body in hot water. She had removed her jacket, inner tunic, and bra. Her back was to him, and she was obviously sure he was still asleep. He decided not to let her know otherwise.

Her motions were efficient and yet graceful. There was something so relaxed about her that he found himself wishing she could be that unconcerned about him at all times. He took a deep breath at last, knowing the time had come for the second phase of his plan to detoxify Katalya Tremain. "Would you like some help with your back?" he inquired.

Across the cave there was a smothered exclamation as Tremain dropped the scrap of cloth she had been using as a sponge and dived for her tunic and jacket. She held the tunic across her bosom and treated Spock to an ample display of invective. He waited calmly until she had run out of new ways to describe him, his habits and ancestors for at least ten generations. He found her vocabulary very impressive, but decided the time had come to put a stop to the activity. "I think you're repeating yourself, Doctor. You've already accused me of that particular perversion once."

"How dare you just lie there and pretend to be

asleep while I was bathing? You know very well I wouldn't want to be unclothed in front of you!" Her voice was shaky with rage.

"I don't at all understand what's bothering you. You have, as near as I can tell, a perfectly acceptable body for a female Terran of your age, social position, and rank in Star Fleet. Of course, I admit I have only seen part of it. I'll reserve judgment until I have seen you completely nude."

Tremain's only response was to wad up her washcloth and throw it at him. She got into her clothes and stalked out of the cave. Spock had a suspicion he would have to hunt for his own vegetables this morning.

14

On board the *Enterprise,* Dr. McCoy had spent an extremely sleepless night. What few interludes of sleep he experienced were made hellish by nightmares about what might be happening down on the surface. In his mind's eye he had seen Tremain kill Spock in at least a dozen exotic ways. Considerably haggard, he made his way to the Bridge to resume his restless pacing.

"Bones, if you keep that up you're going to wear a hole clear through the deck," Kirk said, watching his medical officer with some concern. The Captain knew how much Katalya Tremain meant to McCoy, and he was very worried about the burden of guilt the doctor could so easily assume. "Don't worry, we'll get them out of there all right."

"But I promised her I'd be down there—I told her she could come to me whenever the pressure got too bad—and I've failed her. She's all alone down there." McCoy came to a stop facing Kirk. The Captain could tell from the dark circles under McCoy's eyes what the last night must have been for him.

"She's not entirely alone. But then, I suppose that worries you even more. It worries me." Kirk leaned back in his command chair and tried hard to relax. "I didn't sleep very well either, Bones. I kept thinking about Spock. Do you think she'll kill him?" The question was not an easy one, but it was something Kirk had to know. And it was clear from the expression on McCoy's face that he had been thinking along the same lines.

"I'm not sure, Jim," he said slowly. "But if she's pressured she's perfectly capable of it. Oh God, why didn't that woman let me Sigmund her?"

Spock waited until he was sure Tremain had worked off a little of her aggression by hiking across the hillside in search of breakfast. He then left the cave to follow her, hoping he could finally put an end to the game he was playing.

He found Katalya Tremain almost at the crest of the mountain slope. She was sitting on a large rock with two of the small rabbitlike creatures beside her, and busily plinking away with her phaser at several rocks in the vicinity. She did not look very happy.

Spock moved silently up to a position less than a meter behind her. "That is a considerable waste of energy, Dr. Tremain. I would suggest in the future that you be a little more conservative."

Tremain spun around, her phaser aimed directly at Spock's midsection. He could not tell from where he was standing whether it was set on stun or not. He froze, waiting. Her face was a mask of indecision. She glanced at the phaser, then at him, and back down at the phaser. The moment stretched into eternity.

Finally, with an inarticulate snarl of annoyance, she threw the phaser onto the ground. Spock took a deep breath and relaxed.

"Why in hell did you do that, Vulcan? I could have killed you so easily."

Spock walked slowly forward, bent, and retrieved the phaser. He handed it back to her and she received it silently. "I had to know if you were capable of killing me. And, more important, you had to know."

Tremain looked up at him, startled. "Is that why you've been so cruel? Were you really trying to goad me into killing you? You came very close last night. But I think you know that."

"I did have some suspicion of it, when I noticed

the sound of your teeth chattering and you did not take your phaser and heat the rocks around your bed. I assume you felt it would have been too much of a temptation."

Tremain nodded and looked down at the phaser in her hand. It was set on kill.

"Don't you think that sneaking up on me was taking a considerable risk, after this morning? You were being very annoying, you know."

"No more annoying than you've been since the moment you stepped aboard the *Enterprise*. I felt some sort of test was necessary to establish peace between us. Shall we both cry 'Pax' and be done with it?" Spock sat down on the rock next to her. "I think we can have a serious talk now, Doctor, don't you agree?"

Tremain returned the phaser to its clip on the back of her belt. "I suppose you're right. I have been equally difficult. You, at least, have never threatened to kill me." She glanced at him from under lowered eyelashes.

"I would have found a threat which I had no intention of carrying out to be simply a waste of breath. I admire your work; in fact, I've admired your professional abilities for quite some time. But I'd hoped to eventually be able to say that I admired you as a person."

"I'm sorry I won't be able to return the compliment, Mr. Spock. Precisely what is it you want of me?"

"Some sort of truce. We have no way of knowing how soon the Romulans will land on Arachnae, but our survival may be dependent on cooperation. I am asking for that cooperation. And if you wish you may view it from a totally selfish viewpoint. You might need my help to stay alive."

Tremain appeared to be studying the problem from several angles. "I'm not sure I agree with you. If the Romulans do arrive here, they may kill us on sight. In that case I would be no better off having established some sort of agreement with you than without one."

"I quite agree. But you must keep in mind," Spock reached up and touched the tip of his ear, "that I might have certain natural advantages in dealing with Romulans that you lack."

"I think I see your point," she said.

Spock winced. "That is another advantage to the Vulcan language. A Vulcan is totally incapable of producing a pun, which I consider one of the lowest forms of humor."

"I wasn't aware that Vulcans recognized any form of humor. But I think we may have reached one point of agreement. I also dislike puns, and I didn't mean that one deliberately." She turned and studied his face quietly for a few moments. "All right," she said at last, "I'll agree to a truce. I will try to avoid being too obvious about my dislike of you, and you in return will refrain from sexual innuendo, touching me, or being overly obnoxious. Was that what you had in mind?"

"I think it will suffice for now. But in view of possibly changing conditions, I would not care to be held rigidly to any agreement. I can, however, promise you that I *will* refrain from sexual innuendo. I don't find that sort of sport interesting. I did it to prove a point—that I have a very strong suspicion of where some of your neuroses may lie. Would you care to comment?"

"You don't have a license, or the equipment, to Sigmund, Mr. Spock, and I'll thank you not to try doing it. Add that to the list of conditions."

"Done. Now, let's get on with the business of breakfast. I want to explore that rock outcropping a little more thoroughly. Since we are stranded here, we might as well try to complete our original mission."

Dr. Tremain nodded silent assent. She knew that, were she to speak, she would probably comment, "How like a Vulcan."

The hole in the rocks was large enough for Spock and Tremain to stand stoop-shouldered within it. Spock took out his tricorder and checked the length of the tunnel. "We may have to do a little walking, Doctor, but I think this could be our best chance of finding out a little more about the Arachnians. From past reports there's been no indication that anyone has penetrated as far as their home lairs. I would suggest we attempt to do so. It may be dangerous, but we have very little time to complete our mission."

"About how long do you think it'll be before the Romulans claim this planet?"

"It is extremely hard to predict, but I am taking into consideration the figures we had before leaving the *Enterprise,* and I would say by approximately sundown Arachnae will be well into Romulan space. There is, however, also the fact that this is a relatively large planet, so there is no great likelihood that the Romulans will automatically land in this immediate area. That is why we're maintaining our radio silence, after all—so they won't know where we are. Shall we go forward?"

Tremain nodded and followed the crouched figure of the tall Vulcan deeper into the ground. The walls had a faintly luminescent quality, as though something had been painted onto them. Spock pointed this out, and he and Tremain moved closer to examine it. "It appears to be some sort of lichen," Tremain commented. "I wonder whether it simply grew here, or whether there is a chance the Arachnians planted it."

"If it is cultivated, that would indicate some form of intelligence. But," and Spock looked down at his tricorder, "it does seem to be some form of natural phenomenon. It is feeding on the body fluids left by the action of the horta-creatures in their burrowing. For the moment we can assume that it grows here on its own. Does it provide adequate light for you to see by? I'm hesitant to use the light on the tricorders because I've been concerned about running into a band of Arachnians. You saw what they did to the camp; we wouldn't have much chance of escaping. If we can keep them from knowing we're here, though, we might avoid their company."

"It's a little dim, but I can manage," Tremain replied, accepting Spock's leadership with surprising ease.

They moved slowly along the downward-sloping tunnel. The moss underfoot turned black, as though charred, as they walked over it. Tremain bent to examine the moss with her tricorder and found that the crushing seemed to have killed it. She studied the phenomenon for a moment and then said, "This might serve as a useful guide to where the Arachnians are. We simply look for tunnels that have rubbed areas on the floor. It might also make it easier to follow our path out of here. I think it's a good idea to keep escape always in mind."

She got to her feet, dusted off her hands, and continued down the tunnel. They reached a crossroad and examined the floors of the three off-branching tunnels. One of them was dark along the floor.

"It appears that we will now put your idea to practical use," Spock said. "Shall we go forward?"

Tremain turned around to look down the tunnel toward the opening that could be dimly seen in the distance like a winking star. She sighed slightly and said, "We might as well; that's what we're here for."

The slant of the tunnel became much more severe, and they found themselves having to brace their bodies against the wall to keep from slipping. It seemed to both of them that there were times when it might be advantageous to have the six legs of an Arachnian. As they moved deeper into the earth, Spock noticed an odor in the air, a sickeningly sweet honey scent that they'd first noticed at the campground—only this was many times stronger. He came to a halt and stood listening.

"I believe we're getting fairly close to their dwellings, and I suggest we proceed with caution. Have your phaser ready, but please set it on stun. Also watch for any branching paths; we must at this point consider avoiding any area that might be traveled." He moved forward slowly, listening for the sound of anything coming down the tunnel.

It was Tremain who spotted the narrow cleft in the rocks off to one side. She pointed it out to Spock and they examined it, finding that it was wide enough for them to clamber up a narrow rock chimney which seemed to lead toward the surface. It was a perfect form of natural ventilation.

"We might try that," Tremain said. "It seems to have a side vent leading to a cavelike opening in the middle of this mountain. Even if it isn't what we're looking for, we'll only have lost a little time."

Spock acknowledged this to be so, and with Tremain leading the way they climbed deeper into the mountain. There was less moss on the rocks now, and Spock switched on the light of his tricorder. They seemed to be moving slightly upward from the tunnel they had originally been in. Spock constantly checked the location by means of the tricorder.

The chimney of rock opened out in to a small cave. The walls were damp and the floor several centimeters deep in water. They sloshed through the pool, continuing in the direction of what the tricorder indicated was an extremely large hollow place in the mountain itself.

"I suspect we are approaching the cavern. I would suggest you be as quiet as possible," Spock said, suiting his actions to his words by crouching close to the floor of the cave and moving slowly through the water. They could already smell the sickening honeysweet scent of the Arachnians in the air.

The pool on the floor of the cave had become a stream, and they could see ahead of them a natural arch formation that glowed blue-white. A heavy, wet splashing sound from the stream indicated a waterfall at the lip of the cave. They edged forward, keeping close to the wall until they could peer downward.

They were positioned on a natural observation platform beside the waterfall. And the wonders of the Arachnian home cave were spread below them like a diorama.

The light came from the walls of the immense cavern. They were moss-covered and glowing, but this was the least of the wonders. Below them a city rose, stalactites and stalagmites of limestone tinted rose and blue and violet combined with structures that could only have been made by the Arachnians. It was a fairy tale city of spires and arches and magnificent Gothic cathedral-like structures.

Tremain lay flat on her stomach beside Spock on the floor of the narrow cave, the water splashing only centimeters from her prone body. Short bits of rock cut at her legs and belly, and the walls seemed uncomfortably close. The ceiling was barely high enough above her head to allow room to move—and there was also the uncomfortable fact of Spock's extreme proximity. But the view from their fissure down into the hive was so exciting she could forget for a few moments the presence of a hated Vulcan.

The hive stretched into the far distance and faded into infinity. There were buildings, incredible buildings: Gothic, with towers, flying buttresses, medieval castles—all of them built from blocks of carved stone, mortared together with a substance produced by the Arachnians' own bodies. She and Spock watched, fascinated, as teams of Arachnians hauled rocks into place, using ropes woven from their own hair.

Spock touched Tremain's arm and pointed wordlessly at a group holding aloft one Arachnian which was producing the mortar from its mouth. Its jaws worked frantically as the thick greenish fluid flowed out onto the surface of the wall and seemed to melt into it. Blocks of stone were swiftly placed on top of the mortar, leveled into place, and seemed to set almost instantly. The sight was unbelievable.

Tremain looked down at the base of the hive and gasped. She had never realized, in their careful crawling upward through the fissured rock, how high she and Spock had actually come. The floor of the hive was at least ten stories below them. They would not have to worry about dying at the hands of the Arachnians; should they make a mistake in turning around to leave, the fall alone would kill them. She wanted to reach out and grab Spock's shoulder just to have something to hang onto, but her dislike of him held her back. Spock turned to her, sensing, perhaps, the fear.

"Are you afraid of heights?" he asked.

"No, not precisely," she said in a somewhat trembling voice. "They never would have allowed me in Star Fleet if I were. But there's something about being up here—and looking down there—that is so awe-inspiring."

"Yes," Spock said, looking over the lip of the fissure. "Somewhat like the theaters on Antares. Have you ever been to one? It's a three-dimensional effect, and you can look all around you and see the entire play and all that is involved in presenting it. There is no backstage; you are a part of the drama."

"No, I haven't seen that sort of production, and I don't think I'd care to. It would be too much like life to me. I prefer the safety of knowing that there *is* a backstage."

"But in this instance, Dr. Tremain, we are the backstage." Spock glanced downward again. "Do you have any idea what would happen if they realized we were up here?"

"Yes." Tremain's voice trembled a little. "They'd kill us. And not very nicely. You saw what they did to Williams and Mendoza and the rest of our party. I don't want to die that way. It's so brutal. I've never wanted to die by the hands of something with less intelligence than myself."

"Then you continue to deny that these creatures are intelligent?" Spock said. "I should think their architecture alone would prove they are more than mere

animals. Look at it! Look at that incredible construction. If they were mud hovels, or simply piles of that
mortar, mere coverings, I could believe they were animals—but animals do not create such form, or that
incredibly logical an architectural shape to their dwellings."

"Then you obviously have never studied a spider's
web or the wax in a bee's hive," Tremain pointed out.
"There's the same symmetry, the same beautifully
arched shapes. But a bee or a spider has no concept
whatever of what it is creating. To it, the construction
is simply functional."

"Ah *ha!*" Spock said, gloating. "But you see,
those *are* functional forms. Can you look at those
strange arches and towers down there and really
insist that they are purely functional? I can see no
purpose other than esthetic pleasure involved in building
such complicated structures."

"You're falling into the trap that many zoologists
face. You are giving the animals humanoid characteristics because that is what you want to find. It's a little
like people watching penguins in a zoo and giving them
personalities, when what it really is is a projection of
their own thoughts and desires. Those buttresses and
towers may indeed have a function—we simply don't
know what it is. You want it to be beauty and a sign
of intelligence—and therefore, to you it is."

"And you similarly discount the use of tools,
pulleys, and the fact that they have woven that rope
from their own hair. There is obvious thought there.
They have knowledge of tools, and how to build them."

"Again, I could point to a great number of animals who have similar tool-making abilities. On Earth,
otters use rocks carried on their chests to smash open
clams. On Deneb there is the frogmouth; it builds
elaborate nests utilizing a pulley system made of the
kukulu nut to raise reeds from the ground up into the
tree. There are also the leaf-palace builders of Trachus
—and if you look at those incredible fairylike castles
built entirely of leaves, you might tend to believe that

intelligent beings formed them. But then when you see those little louselike creatures and realize that a billion of their brains could dance on the head of a pin, it becomes ludicrous."

"Doctor, that was a *non sequitur*. Brains cannot dance."

"I'm perfectly aware of that, Mr. Spock, but it amused me. That's one of your problems, one shared by all Vulcans: you are incapable of whimsy. You can't think of anything solely to amuse yourselves. It's something very nasty in you."

Spock looked down at the frayed surfaces of his uniform and ruefully examined one badly torn elbow. He was obviously also searching for some way out of the discussion. For some reason her accusation of a lack of whimsy had upset him. "I think," he said, "we had best consider returning to the cave. It's getting quite late; it will be dark soon, and we'll need what sunlight we have left to make sure we descend safely. Then too, I would not care to be caught in the dark by a returning horde of forager Arachnians."

Tremain nodded, but she was not going to let go of the conversation so easily. "You didn't like the accusation of a lack of whimsy, did you? Why? Because it was true? Or because it wasn't?"

Spock stared off into space for several moments. His eyes were distant, considering. He waited, and then slowly turned to her. "I want to tell you something about my childhood," he said. "Something that I don't think you'll understand because of how you react to Vulcans—but something that is important to me. I was never able to imagine as a child. I was never *allowed* to imagine. Can you understand what that means, or how much joy it has taken out of my life?"

Tremain jumped slightly, banging her head against the roof of the cave. There was a sharp clatter of stones falling from the roof, and both she and Spock froze, waiting to see whether the sound had been noticed. There was no change in the activities of the hive below them. The sound had probably been too high and too distant, or perhaps the fall of rocks and pebbles was a natural sound in this place.

"I don't want to hear about your childhood, Mr. Spock. It's not part of our agreement that I listen to your babblings. I'm not interested in your childhood— it was probably as cold and bleak and unpleasant as you are."

"You're quite right," Spock said. "It was. And it is perhaps why I am."

"I don't see why you bother to tell me these things," Tremain continued with some asperity. "It makes no difference and it's as if you're forcing yourself on me. You're trying to make me look at you as a person, and I don't want to do it. I don't want to accept the fact that you may be a living, breathing being with something going on in your head other than the computerlike twistings of Vulcan thought processes. If I do that, I'll have to admit you're real. And I prefer to think of you as a phantom, as some vile dream that I can get rid of any time—any time I please."

"But you did start the conversation," Spock observed. "And it seemed logical to me to answer your question. And as for getting rid of me, think about this morning and how easy it would have been for you to kill me. I mean, consider: you would not have had any difficulty explaining it once you returned to the *Enterprise*. We've lost ten people already to the Arachnians, so what does one more matter? Captain Kirk would be somewhat suspicious, yet in the end he would have to accept it if there was no proof. Or did you consider that possibility?"

Tremain edged backward, back the way they had come. Her uniform snagged on a rock, and she turned to free it. "Yes, I thought about it," she said. "And I found that I couldn't do it—oddly enough, because of the fact that you're a Vulcan. It would be very easy for me to kill; I've killed before. One can't be a member of Star Fleet as long as I have without having killed. But if I kill *you,* you'll come back. Oh, not alive—I don't believe in that sort or thing—but every night, when I went to sleep, you'd be there. I know you Vulcans, I know what you'd do to the inside of my head—and I know I could not forget you. I may loathe you, wish you dead, I may hope tomorrow that the Arachnians dismember and eat you, but I can't do it myself. This morning's little test proved that, I think, both to your satisfaction and to my own."

Spock nodded, more to himself than to her, and began to edge backward. "Watch out for loose rock," he cautioned. "If you slip and fall, I will have a great deal of difficulty rescuing you."

"Did it ever occur to you, Mr. Spock, that it might be a great deal easier for you if *I* were dead? You wouldn't have to put up with my dislike of you."

"I wish I could get you to understand that your dislike of me doesn't matter in the slightest. It does not change my opinion of you as a brilliant scientist and it does not change my opinion of myself. It does, in some slight way, grieve me, because I see it as a flaw in an otherwise almost perfect mechanism—your mind. And," he said, reaching downward with one foot for a toehold, "I am not entirely sure I believe such a flaw actually exists. I suspect, like Dr. McCoy, that it is perhaps an elaborate cover for something much more involved."

"Oh," she said, chuckling. "Are you going to be chasing red herrings, too? I thought I left Sigmundizing back on the ship. You haven't the equipment for it, not unless you intend to mindmeld—and I'll fight that with every bit of strength in my body. And if you dare to do it, I will present you with images of such nastiness, of such violence, that you will not be able to cope with them. Have you any idea, Mr. Spock, of what might be present in the dark side of a human mind? Would you like to wade hip-deep in the cesspools of the dark side of me? I don't think you'd find it enjoyable."

"No, I probably wouldn't. But I might find it interesting. At the moment though, I think we had better devote the best part of our energies to getting out of here as safely as possible. I would advise you save your breath for the climb downward. I'm afraid that if you work yourself into an emotional state, you may miscalculate and miss a step, and fall. That could prove rather difficult, as I might find myself having to cope with a rather Terran emotion—guilt. What *do* you think of guilt, Dr. Tremain?"

There was no sound from below him except the busy scrambling of the woman down the fissures in the rocks. Spock smiled quietly and wondered what McCoy would think of his methods.

They moved cautiously down the tunnel, back toward the entrance. As they walked, Spock and Tremain continued their argument concerning the intelligence of the Arachnians.

"I'm sure they are intelligent," Spock said, "and once we're able to communicate with them, I think we will be able to persuade them that remaining in the Federation might be best for them."

"*If* they are intelligent, which I doubt." She glanced at him from the corner of her eye, smiling. "I'm rather surprised you're taking an attitude directly opposite that of your father. I thought you Vulcans always stuck together."

"Are you referring to his assumption that they are animals, or his assumption that, intelligent or not, Romulan domination might be better for them than remaining in the Federation?"

"Either way, it's immaterial; you're disagreeing with him, and that's what surprises me."

Spock stopped to check the condition of the moss in the floor of the cave. "We go this way," he said, pointing to a side tunnel. "But there are some indications here of more than just our footprints. I suggest you get your phaser ready, Doctor—we might have a little difficulty getting out onto the surface. And again, set it on stun."

"I notice you didn't answer my question, Mr. Spock," Tremain said as she reached for her phaser.

"I have been in disagreement with my father for a great number of years—that is nothing new. He and I do not always see things with the same eyes, any more than you and I do. That fact does not automatically make one or the other of us right. It's entirely possible, you know, that we're both wrong."

Tremain snorted and commented that this was just one more example of convoluted Vulcan logic. Spock said nothing, but increased his pace. He could see up ahead dim flickerings of light at the cave entrance, and he was not entirely pleased with the flickering effect—which could be caused only by something passing back and forth in front of the opening.

"I think we may be in trouble," Tremain said, looking down the tunnel and seeing the random motions at the entrance. "I don't suppose there's any other way out." She reached for her tricorder, and the machine verified her supposition. This was the only exit within a radius of at least four kilometers.

"Well," she said, "it appears it is forward, forward, dear friends, into the breach, for Harry, England, and St. George." She half-laughed at her own use of so silly a quotation at a time like this.

Spock did not answer, but lengthened his strides toward the mouth of the cave. Behind him Tremain had to run to keep up. There were half a dozen Arachnians gathered at the cave mouth. Spock, phaser on stun, expertly cut them down and then moved out into the sunlight. He half-turned to see that Tremain could negotiate her way over the fallen Arachnians.

That momentary concern for the woman was a mistake. Tremain, from inside the tunnel, saw the shadow of the Arachnian behind Spock. She screamed and fired, but it was a fraction of a second too late.

15

On board the *Enterprise,* Captain James Kirk stood beside the science officer's console watching the chronometers over Chekov's shoulders. The moving figures indicated the time remaining before the leading edge of Arachnae's solar system left the Neutral Zone and moved into Romulan territory. That time was now measured in seconds.

On the monitor screen the lines indicating the Romulan border moved stealthily across the orbit of this system's outermost planet. It was now a moot point whether the Romulans could claim the entire system, although the planet Arachnae itself was still within the Neutral Zone.

There was the sound of a message coming in to the communications board. Lieutenant Uhura picked up her earplug, put it in place, and opened the channel. She listened for a moment, and then said, "Sir, there's a message coming in from the Romulan vessel."

"Put it on the main screen, Lieutenant."

Kirk walked slowly back to his chair and, with the relaxed grace that was so much a part of him, settled into his position of command facing the screen, where the image of a Romulan officer was forming.

Commander Thrax looked coolly confident. "As you no doubt know, Captain Kirk, the Arachnae system has now passed out of the Neutral Zone, into Romulan territory. I now intend to place an exploration

party on the planet. I would advise you not to interfere with them."

"I am sorry, Commander, I can't allow that,"
Kirk's face was equally calm. "The rest of the Arachnae system, including its sun, is still in the Neutral
Zone, which is not Romulan territory. It will not be in
Romulan territory for nineteen more hours. Therefore
you cannot claim this planet; should you attempt to do
so before it is rightfully yours, the results will not be
pleasant." The expression on the Romulan Commander's face made it clear Kirk's threat had been under-
stood.

"I would suggest, Captain, that you contact the
Federation Council. You are an interloper here, and I
think you will find that your Council is more than
willing to let us have the planet without waiting the
necessary nineteen hours. It will be ours eventually."

Kirk knew he could not tell the Romulan Commander the real reason he was unwilling to turn the
planet over. The Federation had to know whether the
beings on Arachnae were intelligent, and so far there
had been no report either confirming or denying that
intelligence. Kirk had to play for time. "Commander,
I will contact the Federation Council. But as you know,
we are far enough from Babel to make it impossible
for any message to reach the Council in less than two
hours. I would therefore need an adequate amount of
time for such a message to reach Babel, be discussed,
and my orders returned to me."

Commander Thrax considered the request.
Finally he nodded and said, "Very well. I will give you
five hours, not one minute more. But the planet is ours,
whether or not the entire system is technically within
our borders. And if you are still in orbit around
Arachnae after the allotted time, I will destroy you."
The screen went black.

Kirk leaned back in his chair and sagged visibly.
He reached up to wipe off the two or three beads of
perspiration on his forehead. He hoped the Romulan

Commander had not noticed them. Five hours was just barely enough time for the Federation to send some sort of message verifying his position. He was tempted to break radio silence and contact Spock's party on the planet's surface, but he realized that his main advantage at the moment—and one of the things keeping those people alive—was that the Romulans did not know exactly where the base camp was. And it would take them considerably longer than five hours to locate it. As far as was known, the Romulan sensors were not as delicate as the Federation's, and could not trace a handful of people. A signal either to or from the surface would pinpoint them immediately. The radio silence would continue.

"Lieutenant, open a channel to Star Fleet and relay the entire tape of my discussion with the Romulan Commander. Notify the ship to remain on red alert, and—we wait."

Lieutenant Uhura hastened to do the Captain's bidding. The Bridge was quiet, everyone on it going about their appointed tasks and, like Kirk, waiting. That silent waiting was interrupted by the loud clattering of an emergency signal from the planet Arachnae. Lieutenant Uhura, her mouth a round *O* of astonishment, flipped open a channel and hastily replaced her earplug. She listened, her surprise turning to one of deep concern.

"They're in trouble down on Arachnae, Captain! Dr. Tremain says Mr. Spock has been attacked and wounded by an Arachnian. She requests permission to beam aboard immediately."

Kirk swiveled. "Contact McCoy. Tell him to get on a channel to Tremain. And get me the Romulan ship!" Kirk waited anxiously while Uhura followed orders.

"Sir, I can't raise the *Decius*. All I can get is an automatic response that repeats, 'Kirk, you have five hours.' Shall I try to break through it?" Her forehead furrowed in concentration as she moved her fingers back and forth across the buttons and toggles of the communications center. Her concern was apparent to everyone on the Bridge.

Captain Kirk slammed one fist into his open palm. "Damn! We've got to get them out of there! We can't have Spock die—I won't have a repeat of Mendoza and the others. I won't have it! Where is McCoy?"

Kirk's question was answered by the sound of the turbolift doors opening. Dr. McCoy burst onto the Bridge, almost running across the space between the door and the command chair. Reaching out, he grabbed Kirk by the shoulder.

"Jim, Jim, we've got to do something. We've got to get Spock and Tremain off the planet. We've got to do something, man! Talk to the Romulans. We can't let them stay down there, they'll die. Tremain doesn't have any medical training, and without help Spock will die like the rest of the party." McCoy punctuated his sentences by vigorously shaking Kirk's shoulder.

Kirk reached up and covered McCoy's hand with his own. "Easy, Bones. I'm doing what I can. Just take it easy, she's going to be all right."

"I'm not worried about Katalya, I'm worried about Spock. We know what happens when a person is attacked by Arachnians—Katalya just described to me the way Williams died. There'll be mounting fever, hallucinations, delusions and—death. And it won't be a pretty death, Jim. I've got to get down to him."

"We're trying to open a channel to the Romulans, but they've got an automatic on that's making it hard for us to break through. I don't dare lower our shields, even for an instant, without getting an acknowledgement from them, or we'd all be sitting ducks. They've given us five hours to go away. They're not entitled to the planet for nineteen hours, but they want it now."

"Then let them have the planet! It's not that important to us—not as important as Spock's life. We've got to get him out of there. Offer to make them a trade —they can have the planet now if we can beam up Spock and Tremain."

Kirk closed his eyes for a moment, then opened them again. "Arachnae might prove to be more important to, the Federation than either Spock or Tremain," he said slowly. "We have our orders. We are to find out whether the Arachnians are intelligent or not before we let the Romulans have the planet. We don't have an answer for that yet. And it is not rightfully theirs for nineteen hours. There are precedents involved here that could have Galaxy-wide impact for centuries to come. I intend to do some horsetrading with Thrax, as you suggest, but I need to know first that the Council will back me. If they say we can let the Romulans have the planet immediately, it simplifies everything; we beam up Spock and Tremain, the Romulans get Arachnae, and that's it. But if the Council says we must hold out for nineteen hours, we'll do it. Spock and Tremain knew their danger; we all knew this mission would not be easy, that it might be dangerous. So I'm doing only what I must—nothing."

McCoy wanted to rail some more about the insanity of their situation and the stupidity of the Star Fleet brass, but the look in the Captain's eyes silenced him. It was a haunted look, the expression of a man to whom duty was everything—more important than his friend's life, more important even than his own. James Kirk knew that his best friend might die because of his inaction, yet his hands were tied by the system he had sworn to obey. He would hold to his orders just as strongly as he would later grieve for his friend. McCoy saw no reason to add to the Captain's burden with useless hysterics of his own.

And the Bridge went back to waiting.

On the planet's surface, Katalya Tremain knelt beside the bleeding body of Mr. Spock. She had examined his wounds. There were three of them, deep slashing cuts across his back which were slowly oozing green blood. She took off her jacket, then removed her tunic and began shredding the blue fabric into long, bandagelike strips. Spock was dazed from the quick-acting poison he'd received from the Arachnian's bite before Tremain's phaser blast could stop the native. She had, as quickly as possible, run to his side and examined him, then set her phaser on kill and destroyed all the Arachnians in the tunnel, as well as the one lying stunned outside on the surface. She had taken no pleasure in the act; it had simply been a cold, methodical necessity—as had the killing of the stunned natives at the base camp.

And now she had to attempt the process of healing, a process which she knew very well was doomed to fail. Spock was not likely to die from the cuts on his back—they were unpleasant, but not terminal. It was the alkaloid poisoning that she worried about, and the strange fever that had come over Williams—the merciless progression of rising temperature, delusion, hallucinations, and death; a screaming, unpleasant death.

She bandaged Spock's back, weaving the torn strips of fabric back and forth around his chest and covering the wounds. She knew her actions would do little good, but there was something comforting about being able to do anything at all.

"Don't die, Mr. Spock," she murmured, more to herself than to the semiconscious Vulcan. "Don't die and leave me alone. I couldn't take that, not again." Spock stirred under her ministrations and groaned. His eyes opened and he focused on her with some difficulty.

"Arachnian?" he croaked in a weary voice.

"Yes. There was one of them on the surface, just past the mouth of the tunnel. Try not to talk or move," she said as he tried to rise. She reached out, took his shoulders and gently pushed him down again. He turned his face sideways, his cheek resting on the pebbled ground.

"It hurts," he said quietly. "May I have something to protect the side of my head? There's a pebble cutting into my cheek." His voice was slurred; he was obviously fighting the pain.

With a slight exclamation of dismay at her own

carelessness, Tremain wadded up her jacket, bent over to lift Spock's head, and eased the fabric under his cheek. "Is that better? I don't want you to move around too much. With Williams, his thrashing only seemed to make the fever worse. Just lie still. If you want water or anything, tell me."

"Why don't you simply walk away, Dr. Tremain? You could, you know. I'm going to die if I'm not beamed up to the ship soon."

"They can't beam us up. They have to keep their shields up because of the Romulans." When Spock failed to reply, Tremain continued, "And as for my walking away from you and letting you die—well, as I said last night about the food, I wouldn't do that to anyone, not even a dog. So I will do what I can for you, I'll stay here beside you, try and help you with the worst of the hallucinations, and wait for them to do something upstairs."

"It might be advisable for you to gather what coverings we have up at the cave and try utilizing them to protect me from the ground. I do find this a bit uncomfortable. In fact, I have a strong suspicion that there is some sort of insect mound in the general vicinity of my ribcage. If I am going to die I would prefer to do it with a little more dignity than having small insects crawling about inside my tunic."

"Mr. Spock, this is no time for levity—and in very poor taste." Dr. Tremain got to her feet and glanced upward toward the cave. "It would take me at least forty-five minutes to get up to the cave and back—if the fever starts, you could do yourself harm thrashing about."

"I had not intended any levity. I meant that as a statement of truth. There *are* small insects inside my tunic. And I do realize that it will take you forty-three-point-six minutes to get to the cave and return. However, I do advise it. Also, you might be able to use some of the blankets to help restrain me. You might also find something to cover yourself as well—or have you lost your excessive modesty, Doctor?"

She looked down at her bare skin and thin transparent bra and smothered an exclamation of dismay. "I did what was necessary—and a true gentleman would have had the kindness not to remark on it. But then, no Vulcan could ever be a gentleman." She was furious at Spock for abruptly breaking their agreement to avoid innuendo.

"Yes, yes, and we will finish this discussion when you return from the cave. Now will you please go?"

Angrily she moved away from Spock at a dogtrot. He watched her go and waited until she was out of visual range. His ruse had worked; she had been made mad enough to stop protecting him and leave. Slowly, painfully, he sat up and glanced in the direction of the Arachnian tunnel opening. He had an idea, a desperate plan that might save his life—and would also answer the Federation's questions about the intelligence of the Arachnians. If he could make his way down the tunnel, find an Arachnian, stun it and mindmeld with it, he might persuade it to help him. Might . . .

16

Spock sat waiting, his back against the wall, facing one of the intersections in the subterranean Arachnian burrow. He could feel his strength ebbing, and the faint teasing of fever at his brain. He had tried searching as far as the ledge overlooking the cavern, and had slowly, painfully, made his way back. He knew he would eventually have only two choices: staying where he was and dying, or making his way to the surface and dying. Neither one was acceptable. There had to be a lone Arachnian somewhere in these tunnels. His tricorder indicated that the tunnel he was facing led into a maze of caverns and exits to the surface. He was hoping to apprehend a returning worker. If he was discovered by a warrior, he would have to make do with that—but a warrior's mind might be far more dangerous for him. He examined his tricorder again and noted a blip which indicated that something was approaching him from the tunnel. He rose slowly to his feet and waited.

The Arachnian skittered out into the crossroads of the tunnel and froze. It turned to face him, and made a high-pitched chittering sound. It started to rear upward onto its hind legs. Spock raised his phaser and stunned it.

He moved slowly toward the fallen being, uncertain for a moment as to how to proceed. If Tremain were right and this creature was an animal, he could be in far more danger than he presently was from the poison. But if it was intelligent, if it was able to understand his problem, then it might be persuaded to save his life. An intelligent race of Arachnians would certainly have an antidote for their own poison.

He moved to its head and examined the large dark brown faceted eyes. There was no indication whatever that they were anything more than the eyes of an insect. There was a faint stirring of doubt in his mind. But he knew that death was not far enough away to make any other form of rescue likely. He had no other choice.

He sighed, reached out, and placed his hands one on each side of the creature's head.

On the surface, Katalya Tremain returned from the cave, arms laden with the blankets and torn shreds of material. She saw that Spock was missing from the place where she had left him, and she dropped the blankets and ran toward her jacket lying creased and dirty on the ground. "Spock! Spock!" she called. There was no answer. She called his name again, and again there was no answer. Lifting her tricorder, she adjusted it to search for Vulcan life forms. After a moment she obtained a reading—Spock was moving down the Arachnian tunnels.

She cursed aloud and pulled out her communicator to signal the ship. "Captain, Mr. Spock is missing. I have a suspicion he may have gone into the Arachnian tunnels. I'm going to have to go in after him."

She waited, listening to Kirk's reply. He had nothing new to tell her—simply a reiteration that the Romulans would not allow anyone to be beamed up, and his orders to find Spock if she could.

"I'll do my best, Captain. I really will." She closed the communicator and put it away. Lifting the tricorder screen once more into position, she began tracking the missing Vulcan. "Damn you, Spock! If you've mindmelded with one of those things, you deserve exactly what you're going to get. . . ."

At first Spock found only the initial resistance to telepathic contact that any mind possessed. Then he was past the walls of resistance and into the actual thoughts of the Arachnian. Suddenly he was flooded by impressions of food-gathering and the joy of successful root-grubbing. His own mind recoiled in horror. The Arachnian *was* an animal—basically primitive, unevolved and unable to reason for itself.

Spock tried to pull himself back, but it was too late. His strength was sapped by the poison in his system, and his mind was overwhelmed, swamped, by one all-consuming thought: a repeated chant of *Home, home, home,* monotonous and demanding.

He retreated out of the Arachnian's brain, and tried to overcome the instinctive reactions with his own Vulcan logic—but the chant of *Home, home, home* was too compelling. He clutched at his head, as if to squeeze reality back into it; but the chant went on—covering, engulfing, any thoughts of his own. Without being aware of it, he screamed—the sound of a soul in torment.

Tremain found him lying beside the body of the stunned Arachnian. At first she mistook his monotonous chanting for the beginnings of the hallucinatory phase of his illness, but quickly changed her mind. As she knelt beside him and examined the tricorder for indications of how his fever was progressing, she found his temperature far lower than she'd expected. "Spock. What is it? What have you done? Did you mindmeld with that beast?"

"Home. Home. Home. Animal. It's—home, home —an animal." Spock was struggling with his last strength to get out some sort of explanation. His hold on his own mind was tenuous.

Tremain got to her feet, took her phaser and destroyed the Arachnian that lay beside Spock. The Vulcan screamed in agony, his eyes glazed and he could not—or would not—focus on Tremain. Grabbing him by the shoulders, she pulled him roughly to his feet.

"Come on. Let's get you out of here." She

pushed him in the direction of the tunnel entrance. He stumbled, righted himself, and began walking toward the surface.

Suddenly he stopped and turned to face her. "You are not of the hive. Not of the hive. Home. Home. Home." Then for a moment his face took on its normal expression, but once again went blank. With a great deal of effort, Spock pulled himself together and said, "Help me. Please. Help me. I must—home—home—home—" He moved like a sleepwalker toward Tremain. Roughly he shoved her out of the way and began to move downward, in the direction of the main cavern.

On the ground behind him, Tremain pulled herself up on one elbow, drew her phaser and stunned him. It would be very difficult pulling him to the surface—but that would be far easier on her conscience than allowing him to continue downward into the main hive where, since he was not actually a member but only thought he was, the warrior Arachnians would tear him apart for being "not of the hive."

The trip to the surface was a nightmare Tremain hoped never to experience again. It seemed an eternity of pulling Spock slowly up the inclined tunnel. Her body was bathed in sweat, and Spock's uniform was a torn and tattered parody of itself, but she had managed it. She wrapped him in the blanket scraps and turned her phaser on its maximum setting, playing the beam back and forth across the mouth of the tunnel until the outcropping of rocks was nothing more than a heap of slag. She then decided it was time to contact the ship.

"Lieutenant Uhura," she said when she received a response, "Spock's in bad shape. He's mindmelded with an Arachnian and I think he's trying to tell me that they are animals, but I can't be positive. He's trapped with an alien mind, and I don't know how accurate his observations are or what I can do for him.

Get McCoy, get him down here any way you can. Tell the Captain he's got to do something!"

Aboard the ship, James Kirk was gaining a full realization of what the word "powerless" could mean. Lieutenant Uhura had been trying ceaselessly to reach the Romulan ship. There had been no answer; they were still refusing communication. There was nothing Kirk could do. It was too early to expect any communication from Star Fleet, there was no way to drop the shields and get McCoy down to the surface without inviting destruction by the Romulans, and there was nothing he, Kirk, the best starship captain in the Federation, could do personally.

He wanted to hit out at something, kill, destroy, maim—anything to prevent this overwhelming feeling of inadequacy. Dr. McCoy had ceased pacing and simply stood beside the command console in stony silence.

"Do something, Bones," Kirk snapped. "Come up with something. Some sort of answer for Tremain down there. When Spock comes to, she's going to have a lot on her hands."

"All I can tell her is to keep him under. I'm tempted to suggest she bash his head with a rock, because if she keeps using a phaser to stun him repeatedly she'll end up destroying every brain cell he's got." McCoy's voice was distant and dreamy; the strain was beginning to tell on him as well. "Isn't there some way we can get through to the Romulans, Jim? If, as Katalya says, the Arachnians are animals, our job is over. Let those bloody Romulans have it—planet, Arachnians, graves, and all."

"Snap out of it, Bones. I'm doing what I can. And if they don't answer our signal soon, by God I'll lob a photon torpedo across their bow." Kirk swiveled to face Uhura. "Lieutenant, put up the gain as high as you can. I don't care if you blast the drums out of their pointed ears, but make sure they get the message that the planet is theirs. I'm giving it to them because I'm sure the Council will back my decision. And if it doesn't . . . then to hell with the Federation, I'm doing it anyway."

On board the *Decius*, Maximinus Thrax glumly listened to the message from the *Enterprise* while Licinius paced the deck. "What do you make of it, sir?" the younger man asked. "It sounds as if the Federation is willing to give us the planet—and it isn't even in Romulan territory yet."

"It's not like Kirk to give in this easily. I wonder if it's a trick. I'm not sure what to do. Everything we've been taught about that man indicates that any message from him is absolutely untrustworthy. No, I think we wait. Do not answer the communication, and we will see what the Federation Council says in answer to Kirk's message to them."

"Sir," Licinius moved toward the communications panel. "They're sending another message to the Federation. Something about the beings on Arachnae possibly being nonsentient. Kirk is asking for instructions. Should we give them more time for an answer to that message?"

Thrax rubbed his eyes and looked up at his viewscreen, which showed an image of the *Enterprise* hanging in space. "If only I knew what Kirk was up to. If only he could be trusted, this could solve our problems. If only Kirk could be trusted."

On the surface of Arachnae, Tremain sat beside Spock's unconscious body. She had had to use the phaser again on the Vulcan when he had begun to regain consciousness and struggled with his bonds. She knew she could not go on stunning him—it would be too destructive to the nervous system. She was also aware that she could not cope with him fully conscious.

Even in a half-awakened state, Spock had tried to move in the direction of the now-cooling rocks. He had simply murmured over and over again, "Home.

Home. Home." It was obvious that the mind and instincts of the Arachnian were taking over, and that there was very little of the Vulcan left.

If she had to shoot him again, perhaps it would be more merciful to set it on kill. That was a thought that she found herself disliking very much. There were memories in her mind that kept crowding their way to the forefront—memories she didn't like and did not want to consider. She glanced again at Spock, drew out her communicator and flipped it open. *"Enterprise,"* she said, "get me Dr. McCoy." She waited until McCoy came on and said, "I don't know what to do, Len. He's going to die, either from the fever or from what's happening in his mind. He can't survive this. Isn't there anything that can be done up there?"

"We're doing everything we can, darling." McCoy's voice was thin and unfortunately very far away. "Jim is considering dropping the shields and beaming the two of you up anyway. He feels that the gesture might make the Romulans believe we're serious about getting you two off the planet."

"He can't do that!" Tremain clutched the communicator in anxious terror. "You can't trust the Romulans, they're worse than Vulcans. They'll destroy the *Enterprise* if you drop the shields! That won't work. The Captain will have to come up with something else. We're not worth risking the ship for, Len. I mean that."

"Then there isn't anything else. It's either beam you two up or leave Spock to die. Not a very nice choice, I'm afraid. Jim's doing what he can." McCoy sounded almost as though he was trying to reassure himself more than Tremain.

"What about the Federation? Has he told them we think the Arachnians are nonsentient?"

"We sent a message, but it will take a couple of hours before we get an answer—and the Romulans aren't going to give us that much time."

Tremain knew that whatever happened down here on the planet's surface, she would hold herself responsible if Spock died. She had to come up with a solution. McCoy had made it quite clear that there was no help to be gotten from the *Enterprise*. "There is one chance," she said reluctantly. "It's something that I don't even want to think about, but it may be a chance for Mr. Spock. He mindmelded with an Arachnian, and he's getting some sort of instinctive call to come back to the hive. He can't seem to combat it. What he needs is some sort of counterirritant to that call. Something that will strengthen his own instincts as a Star Fleet officer."

Tremain did not want to give voice to the thought in her mind. She was hoping almost that McCoy would pick up on what she was suggesting. She would rather McCoy should say it and deny it than have to be responsible herself. But when silence ensued, she knew she would have to continue. "You see, it was a mindmeld, Len, that got him into this position, and it may take a mindmeld—"

"Katalya, you're crazy! You can't be thinking of mindmelding with a Vulcan! Do you have any idea what that would do to you—or to him, for that matter? Spock would find himself wallowing in your hatred—and if he's in the condition you say he is, he would have the choice of being an animal or going mad with self-loathing. What are you trying to do to him and yourself?"

"Then get us out of here. Make Kirk do something, or I won't have any choice. I don't want to do it any more than you want me to. The idea makes me sick. There's so much . . . there's so much in myself that I would have to face if I did it. But give me another solution. Please, Len! Give me another solution!"

17

Spock could feel himself rising upward toward consciousness. There was the effect of daylight slowly seeping into his brain. His mind accepted awareness. Then the sound of the hive-call began to echo through his mind. It started to drown out his thought patterns. He struggled with it and was able to reduce the volume somewhat by utilizing ancient Vulcan mind-control techniques. But the message of the incessant chanting was there, every pathway to sanity blocked by the command to come home to the hive. He tried to think of his own home on Vulcan; the image superimposed instead was that of the caverns below. He struggled to keep the memory of his father's face, but it faded to that of an Arachnian. He began repeating to himself the Vulcan code of honor; it became tenuous, wispy as morning fog, disappearing before the heat of the hive's demands.

He cried aloud in garbled Vulcan, and felt someone or something touch his face. There was a voice, very far away, speaking a language he could not exactly recognize. It was a woman's voice. His mind fastened onto that sound and tried to follow it. It was vague and distorted. Something inside him said, "Tremain." A memory fitted that name. A woman—a Terran—something about Vulcans. She liked, disliked, Vulcans. He couldn't remember which. It was too confusing, and the hive call was too strong.

Her voice was louder. She was shouting in his ear. He tried to listen, but the hive call reduced it to the squeak of a mouse. The fever was mounting uncontrolled; he could feel the heat licking at the corners of his mind. He was surrounded by distractions. Fever heat, hive chant, and this woman, calling to him. If they would all leave him alone, he reasoned, he could find himself somewhere inside. If they would all just leave him alone.

The woman was saying something over and over. She had to be stopped. She was the one thing he could stop. He tried raising his arm, an action which should have been incredibly easy, but now it seemed as though he must tell each individual muscle strand what to do. Slowly, laboriously, he could feel the hand rise, but the woman had captured it, touching it to her own face. Her voice was louder, demanding. There was a word she kept repeating over and over. It became a counterchant to the cry of "Home." Then it became part of the chant. "Home. Mindmeld. Home. Mindmeld."

They were both commands, and he had to follow them. He was not sure why, but he had to follow them. He tried sitting up. He would go home. But he found he could not move. It was not the puny restraints—he had easily broken the restraint on his hand when he lifted it—but it was the growing inertia of his body, the refusal to obey his commands. He realized he was not voicing those commands properly. Something in him kept insisting he had six legs and a golden down-covered body, and he could not give the appropriate commands to the body he *was* in.

He could not go home. Therefore he must follow the other command. Mindmeld. He freed his other hand and with a great deal of effort reached upward until that hand also rested on the woman's face. His fingers felt for the nerve pressure points at temple, nose, and ears. He found them easily. But would he be able to break through the barriers? Did he have the strength? The command to mindmeld was becoming stronger, and something within him said Yes, this is the right thing. This is what you must do.

He was unsure which part of him the voice had come from—the part that was now increasingly Arachnian, or that dim small part which insisted he was Vulcan. It did not matter; some part of him had agreed to the command. He would mindmeld.

The Spock/Arachnian paused to remember how mindmelding was accomplished and in that moment of thought the Spock mind became for the instant the dominant of the two. He had his hands—Vulcan hands—on Tremain's skin, fingers touching the temporal, zygomatic, and buccal nerve branches on each side of her face. He was ready to mindmeld.

The Arachnian part of him resisted. It too had a memory of mindmelding, and it was not a pleasant one. It struggled for dominance and as the mindmeld progressed a third element was added. Not Tremain's mind —he was not yet in contact with it—but some form of willpower in her that was reaching out to him/them. The Arachnian fled from the touch of the woman who had killed it, but its hold on Spock, still strong, dragged him with it into a ghostlike state of nonbeing. The Arachnian was dead and, to some extent, so was he. There was no Spock, no foodgathering Arachnian— there was only a mind wiped clean and waiting to experience what might lie beyond the threshold of Katalya Tremain's initial resistance to his Vulcan presence.

There was resistance. A feeling of nausea at the contact with him. Then recognition of the fact that he was not Spock, but some neutral being entering her conscious mind.

Are you Spock? someone, probably Tremain, inquired of him.

I—I don't know. I am here, and I must mindmeld with you.

Are you sure you're not the Arachnian? Where is he, already in my mind? There was a touch of panic at the thought of contact with the beast.

No, he's gone. There was a dim cry of "home" from somewhere far away, but it was fast fading into nothingness. *I am alone.*

I don't want a Vulcan in here.

He shimmered and shook with the force of her pain, and then coalesced again into himself. *But you asked me to do this. You commanded it.* He was calm, awaiting her next command.

There was a brief storm, lightning cracked in his vicinity, and thunder followed quickly in its path.

He waited.

The storm cleared and he could see a wall built of durasteel, bright and hard, rising upward as far as he could see. There was a door, and he knew he possessed a key that would open it. But he must have her permission first.

Shall I enter? he asked politely.

The wall vanished, leaving a brick and mortar barrier.

Enter. The word was a sigh of resignation.

He approached the barrier and reached out to place his fingers on it, knowing that his touch was enough to make it crumple.

It resisted. The barrier was strong, but then something within the mind was pushing at it to aid him in his efforts. And it crumbled away at the joint onslaught. The now-open mind was receptive and waiting. He passed over the broken barriers and entered the plains of Tremain's consciousness. It stretched in gray waves to the horizons, undulating fields of memories. Some were barren, blasted by lightning. Others were thick with tombstones; memories of dead dreams. He glided over the meadow of her childhood and knew the feel of a fuzzy pink blanket, tasted the blue ear of a beloved teddy bear. He realized with profound relief that he had left behind at the barriers the entities that had fought over him. He was now neither Vulcan nor

Arachnian. He was Katalya, a young Terran woman.
She/he moved past her/his growing years, the years of
awakening, sensed the bitterness of her unrequited
loves, felt the joys of small successes dancing across
her/him. The lands ahead were darkening; there were
flashes of tragedy, pain. There was a valley of incredible
bleakness, marked with boundary signs. Its name
was Jeremy. The valley was empty. There was nothing there except a faint hint of regret. The darkness
slowly began to surround her/him. She/he found her/
himself racked by the pain of her/his parents' deaths.
She/he felt the deep waters of guilt closing over her/
him. It was dark, so very dark. There was no time, no
feeling, and no further need of gender. Only *it* remained.

It wanted to turn back, wanted to escape from
the enveloping cold, but there was no escape. There
was only the dark behind *it*. In fact, the concepts of
front, back, up, down, were all lost. There was nothing
but blackness, cold, and the feeling of descent, deeper
and deeper into *its* private hell. *It* knew this was *its*
final resting place. *It* would die in the blackness, the
dark, the quiet.

It would be alone in it.

There was nothing.

It found *itself* curling inward, searching for something, something to hang onto, something warm, something real, something that would make *it* aware of *its*
existence.

There was the darkness.

It was no longer moving. *It* was still, silent in the
void. Soon *it* would no longer be. There was nothing to
be for. There was now no memory left even of *its* journey; and the memory of being Katalya, and what Katalya was, was fast escaping. The small grain of being
that was *itself* was almost destroyed. *It* was spreading
itself thin on the darkness, searching.

Somewhere off in the infinite distance, *it* touched
the edge of light. Engrams spread the message quickly:
there was light, there was something, there was reality.

It could not move toward the light, the brightness was coming forward rapidly.

It waited.

The light became visible, tiny like a distant star, but bright—oh, so bright. Moving, spreading a tail of comet's light across the darkness. The dark receded. *It* reached upward for the light, knowing that the light would help *it* regain a sense of selfhood, of gender.

The radiance was all around *him,* glowing, magnificent. *He* found that *he* could see into the heart of the light. Standing there facing *him,* clothed in brightness, was a Vulcan.

The Vulcan's face was a thing of such radiant beauty he could not bear to look at it, nor could he look away. There were the upswept eyebrows, the pointed ears, the deep, compelling eyes and the angular features of a Vulcan. Slowly a name formed: the name Selik. The Vulcan was named Selik. He moved toward it, reaching, feeling himself washed with a deep, abiding love for this Vulcan. He was again one with Katalya; she was reaching. They were reaching. They touched the perimeters of the golden light and were a part of it. They touched Selik and they were a part of him.

They were. They were Selik.

The light was everywhere. There was no sign of darkness any longer. And they bathed in the radiance of love. Their love for Selik. But they were Selik. And they loved.

There was a closeness, a warmth. It was closer than two beings could ever be. They were one. He was Selik, she was Katalya; she was Selik, he was Katalya. And they were together. There was no barrier now. No Vulcan pride, no Terran pride; they were one as they had been meant to be. They knew each other and were content. The radiance slowly coalesced back into Selik-Spock. He found himself standing with Tremain on the Bridge of a ship: the *Calypso.*

"Why?" she asked. "Why did you never let this happen to us while you were alive? I could not live without you. I had to destroy myself in the end. Why did you die and leave me alone to bear the guilt?"

"I did what had to be done. I did not do this to hurt you. I did not want your parents to die with me. But I had no choice." Memories flooded them: being on this ship; working together; seeing each other day after day; being members of a team. A team that was the *Calypso*.

"But it was not like this," he protested. "I did not feel this way. I was not allowed to." His voice was filled with wonder. "I couldn't. Being a Vulcan, I could not love you. You knew that."

"Of course. And that's why I didn't tell you. That's why I kept it inside and never said anything. I didn't want to hurt you." She reached out to him and gently traced the outline of his ear with one finger. "I loved you too much to do that to you. And I'm glad that I didn't. It only would have caused you pain and embarrassment."

"There's no embarrassment now; what we've done goes beyond the simple regulations of my life. I need to give you this. I needed to give you back your life. It's a debt, Katalya."

"Yes, and now I am in your debt. It's a never-ending pattern, isn't it? Of owing and receiving, giving and not giving. What are the parameters of my debt?"

"You can let me go. If you let me become just a memory, it will not be a bitter one. I must be one of the tombstones in your memory field. Selik must become neither light nor darkness, pain nor joy. I must be your past, not your present. You cannot return to this again." He paused, trying to separate in himself the individual components of his mind. There was no hive-cry any more; it was gone. There were two beings who made up himself: there was Selik and there was the Other. And she must do something for the Other. Selik was dead; there could be no debts to a dead Vulcan. But there was a debt to the Other. The Other had brought Selik and Katalya together. Therefore she must do something for the Other. "Find out what he needs,

Katalya. Find out what he wants. You owe him the debt."

"What if he wants *me?* My feelings about Vulcans are so mixed. I had to hate you, you see—it was the only way to stop loving you. It was the only way to stop the pain of remembering what I had never had." She laughed, a bitter sound. "I was remembering what I had never had, and I could not stand the pain that I had no right to feel. I had to hate you instead, and I had to hate all of your race so the pain could not hurt me again. Loving a Vulcan is a disease; once it has been caught it is very easy to catch again with another Vulcan. I had to immunize myself with hatred. That was a wall, a shield, against love. And because I could not love a Vulcan, I couldn't love anyone—not Stone, not McCoy. But here and now I can love you and, in time, lose the hatred. You've given me the gift of love back again."

"I didn't." Selik turned and smiled at her, the beloved face that she had never seen smile. "Don't credit me. I did not do it for you. He did. The Other. And if he demands your love, you must give it. And if he demands you never speak that love or show it, you must do that, too. You owe him yourself. Now go and do what you must. We will never meet again, but you will know that in this time, in this place, for some brief moments I did love you."

She lowered her head to hide the tears. "I could come again—he and I know the way to this place. It could happen again, here inside my memories."

He reached out and gently placed his hands on her shoulders. "It can't, Katalya." His voice was filled with regret. "You can't let it happen. You cannot spend the rest of your life loving a ghost. There are those out there who will offer you love, more love than a ghost can offer you. I am not real. I am only a dream, something you wish had happened. There is no reality to this, no logic, nothing but your imagination. Do not dream your life away, Katalya. Live in the real world. You must accept it and you must not come back here.

I know you are strong enough to do that. Because if you come back you will destroy yourself, and you will destroy me as well. Loving a ghost can be addictive. Necrophilia of the mind, my dear, can be far more lonely than simple masturbation. Go out and love, Katalya. And do not come back."

She would not look at him. Katalya turned and walked away. He watched her fade out into the distances of her mind and knew she was gone. Soon he, Selik, must go. The Other would remain.

"You will be a part of her too, you know," he said to the Other. "You will go out to the land of the living and inhabit your body again. She will have a memory of you, and you will have a memory of her. What you do with it is your own concern. But remember, she does owe you something. Now you must go."

The Other separated from him and stood facing him, and Selik realized that he, too, must go. He looked up and faced the Other, and smiled in recognition. "Goodbye, Spock," he said. "Try to remember me as she does. I wasn't really this handsome, or this brilliantly bright. You're seeing me through her eyes. Remember; and remember me."

Selik was gone. Spock stood alone on an empty Bridge. He looked around at it, accepted what had happened, and then drifted away out of her mind. In the real world he would have to have a long talk with Katalya Tremain.

18

The drifting coalesced. Reality returned slowly. Katalya Tremain found herself lying on the ground, tightly held in Spock's arms. Her head rested on his shoulder; his hand was caressing her cheek. She glanced downward at their entwined bodies, then back up at his face. He was watching her, a quizzical expression in his eyes.

"It was real, wasn't it, Spock?" she asked, hope in her voice. "He was here—Selik—for a few moments . . ."

"No, Katalya, it was only your mind, nothing else. I have seen this sort of thing before in other mind-melds. It is as if your mind is a stage and the various parts of your personality become the actors. I was there because I had become a part of you, but Selik was only your memories of him. The subconscious has many ways of receiving and sorting data that the conscious mind cannot cope with or understand. What you saw in your mind was, to the best of your knowledge, what might have happened between you and Selik if your relationship had continued. It is my opinion that your view was probably close to truth; in time, Selik would have realized what you could mean to him.

"But that ending was left incomplete and your mind has now completed it for you. Selik is dead. He has been dead for quite some time. What we experienced was not a ghost, not something from the other side of death. It was only your own mind. Accept that." Spock knew he had to make that point exceedingly clear to her; if she became convinced that it had been Selik's ghost reaching across the void to her, she could indeed spend the rest of her life seeking to find that ghost again. She had to understand that it had all been simply her own mind providing her with the only logical end to a relationship with Selik.

"But that doesn't mean what happened wasn't true, does it? Do I still owe you something? He said I did, and he told you that, too, after I left the Bridge."

"Oh, it was true; that is, it was true in your reality. But the very fact that you know about his conversation with me proves that he was a part of you. How else would you know what was said in your absence?"

Spock shifted position. He drew his arm away and tried to sit up, wincing at the pain in his back; then, deciding that such an action was illogical, he again relaxed on the ground, pulling the scraps of his torn tunic into place. "I think before I can answer any more questions concerning Selik's reality, I must have a better understanding of precisely what the situation was on the *Calypso*. Will you tell me about it?"

"It's very difficult. It's something I spent a long time forgetting." Tremain turned over so that she did not have to face Spock. "My marriage to Jeremy was over in all but name long before we ever became crewmembers on the *Calypso*—and like a lot of other very foolish women before me, I made the mistake of falling in love with a Vulcan. But I pride myself in having a little more sense than Christine Chapel. For one thing, I never oozed emotionality at him. And when he died, I think I regretted that I hadn't told Selik I loved him—and I resented the fact that he hadn't at least guessed it."

"He may well have known, Katalya. We Vulcans are a great deal more sensitive to the feelings of those around us than we're given credit for. I suspect he knew; and I am sure he respected your silence. It was a great gift you gave him. By not telling him of your love, you allowed him to be what he was—Vulcan. I honor you for that in his name."

"But you don't understand. Had he known, what happened on the *Calypso* might never have happened. You see, it was so close, rescue was so close, there was a chance the *Calypso* could have been saved. But Selik preferred to destroy it. If I had been there, I might have been able to change his mind. I was the expert on biology. I might have been able to find an answer, to destroy whatever those parasites were without destroying the whole ship—and he might have, for my sake, waited a little longer. Then Jeremy would still be alive, and my mother and father—and *he* would still be alive. Do you realize, Spock, the rescue ship came along twenty-two hours after Selik destroyed the *Calypso*? I might have been able to persuade him to let me try to save us all. It's my fault the *Calypso* was destroyed; it was my fault because I couldn't stand to be close to him any more and didn't ship out on that last voyage. I wasn't there to save everyone. And even if I could not have stopped the parasites, I still should have been there with him at the end."

Spock reached out, grasped her shoulder and turned her gently to face him. "No, Katalya. A Vulcan's mind is a curiously structured thing. How could you possibly feel, once he had made the logical decision, that your emotions would have swayed him in the slightest? How could you possibly believe such foolishness?"

"Not emotionalism—logic! I would have used my own logic on him. Spock, there is more than one brand of logic. You Vulcans have never been able to understand that. There are possibilities, there are chances, there is the risk factor to be considered. You have so locked yourselves into your own brand of thought that you've refused to understand the variables. Anything can be proved by logic. I could have spent that time arguing with him; I might have convinced him—"

"And you might have died with him. I read the records of the *Calypso*'s destruction, and my decision would have been precisely the same as Selik's. The life support system was failing, the parasites were multiplying, and there is the distinct possibility that even twenty-two hours, thirty minutes, and eight seconds would have been too long. The rescue ship might still have found the *Calypso* a lifeless hulk—or, even worse, had the parasites transfer their attentions to it. Selik, by his logical decision, saved everyone on that ship from an agonizing death and saved the rest of the Federation from invasion as well. He did what he had to do. Your presence there would have made no difference; no one, not even you, could have stopped that attack in time to avert the damage to the ship. It was too late. By the time the damage was discovered, even if you had killed the creatures the ship would still have been doomed and Captain Selik's decision would have been exactly the same as it was.

"But more importantly, looked at from our present perspective, it *makes* no difference where you were. They're gone, Katalya, and no amount of torture, no amount of hatred—either for yourself or for the Vulcan race—will change that fact. The dead are dead."

Tremain stared past him, looking at some point in time far distant. Tears gathered in the corners of her eyes and trickled slowly down her face. "He might have risked it though, Spock. But he refused to take the risk, refused to be imaginative enough to consider the possibilities. I could have functioned as that imagination, that intuitiveness. I might have persuaded him. . . ."

Spock sighed deeply, both for Katalya Tremain and for his own weariness. He was too tired to continue arguing with her. The pain was bad. His back still throbbed as though lacerated by a whip of fire; the poisons were still in his system, sapping his strength. There were no hallucinations, there would be no madness; mindmelding with both the Arachnian and Tremain had somehow prevented that. But he knew it was still very possible he would die from these wounds. Before his death he had to do something for this woman. "You must stop believing that. I know a part of you will always feel guilty, but you must not dwell on it. There is a future, Katalya, a future for you—and hating Vulcans merely robs you of it. The past is empty, gone, and there is no further need for you to live in it. Go out and look for a future, Katalya. Selik would have wanted that."

Spock closed his eyes and applied Vulcan relaxation techniques to help him ease the physical pain. He knew he would have to conserve his strength; he knew he must rest. "I want you to put a stop to your hatred. You do not honor the memory of the man you loved by hating his people. Promise me you will try to stop the hatred—because if I die here, that may be the only way you can pay the debt you owe to Selik and myself."

"It would take a long time, and there would be times when I would find it very easy to slip back into hating all of your people—but you can't die, Spock. You must live. I can't go through it again. I can't go through having Selik die again, and that is what your death will mean to me. If you want the hatred to stop, don't *die*, Spock!"

"I really have no intention of it, if it can be avoided. I intend to place myself in a state of semi-consciousness to conserve the energy that is left in me. Do not concern yourself if my pulse and respiration drop considerably. I will live as long as I can." He reached out again and touched her cheek, a gesture of benediction. "But stay with me," he said. "Whether I live for an hour, or a day, or a week, stay here with me. I do not wish to die alone." His hand fell back; he closed his eyes and began adjusting his breathing and pulse rate. He had not needed reassurance from her that she would be there. The expression on Tremain's face had been enough for him. He would not die alone; she would be with him until the end.

19

The Bridge of the *Enterprise* was quietly subdued. Emotionally, the wake for Mr. Spock and Katalya Tremain had already started. All that was lacking to the funereal atmosphere was the presence of their dead bodies. Kirk sat hunched in his command chair, his hands lying relaxed in his lap. The time for fist-pounding and shouting was long past.

Beside him, Dr. McCoy had stopped his endless pacing. The only sign of agitation within the doctor was his occasional questioning glances at Uhura.

"Have you heard anything from the surface yet?" McCoy asked. "Is he still alive?"

Uhura shook her head. "The last three signals were not answered, sir. Whatever's happening down there, they're not telling us."

"Try again, Lieutenant." Kirk's voice sounded as though it was echoing from the bottom of a sepulcher. "Try again to raise them."

The lieutenant again signaled the planet's surface, expecting no reply. It came as a considerable shock when the signal was answered by Dr. Tremain. The effect of the biologist's voice was startling. Uhura jumped as though she had touched a live electrical connection. "She's alive!" the lieutenant shouted. "Dr. Tremain's alive. I'm getting a message."

"Put it on an open channel so the entire ship

can hear it," Kirk demanded, swiveling in his chair. "Let's hear that message, Uhura. Find out if Spock is all right, and find out what the situation is down there. Quickly, woman, move!"

The funereal atmosphere faded rapidly as Katalya Tremain's voice filled the Bridge. She rapidly apprised Kirk and McCoy of the fact that she was safe, but that Spock was in dire need of medical attention. She explained the events of the past hour, trying to be as impersonal as possible. She reassured McCoy that Spock was sane, but that he must be gotten back up to the *Enterprise*.

In his command chair, Kirk listened intently to every word the woman was saying. "Then Spock is convinced that they are animals, Dr. Tremain? There's no doubt of that, they *are* animals?"

"No doubt whatsoever, sir. Spock verified that with his mindmeld. They're nothing more than some kind of hive creatures like ants. They're not our concern any more."

An expression of resolution settled on Kirk's face. "Thank you, Dr. Tremain. You've made my choices a little easier. Prepare to be beamed up in a few minutes. Kirk out."

Without bothering to explain further, he turned to Lieutenant Uhura. "I want a message beamed to the *Decius* immediately. They probably won't acknowledge it. They don't really have to; I know damn well they're listening. I'm getting tired of playing 'After you, Gaston.' One way or another, we're going to break this deadlock."

Uhura grinned at her transformed Captain and immediately opened a hailing frequency set as high as she could manage. Kirk cleared his throat and began his speech.

"Now hear this, you pointy-eared excuse for a commander! We've both been pretending that the planet down there is valuable. It isn't. If you want the damned thing, it's all yours. The Federation has given me the authority to dispose of it, and I am ceding it to you in the name of the United Federation of Planets. There is no intellligent life on Arachnae other than my two remaining crewmembers, so you're more than welcome to that cesspool of mindless grubbers. I'm not even convinced that *your* presence on Arachnae will qualify it as having intelligent life.

"But there is one thing I want, and you are going to give it to me. Two of my crewpeople are down there, and others lost their lives while we were playing our charade. Each of us has been afraid to let up and show any sign of weakness—and our pride has been our greatest weakness. Because of it, people have died, and more people may if action is not taken immediately.

"I am going to take that action. Trust has to begin somewhere, and it's going to start with me. I am going to let down my shields and beam up my two remaining crewmembers, and then I shall take my ship and depart. I am going to trust you not to fire on us while we are completing our humanitarian service. And do you know *why* I'm going to trust you?" Kirk paused and gave his adversary a tight-lipped grin. "Because if your weapons show even the slightest flicker of energy while I'm beaming my people up, the *Enterprise* is going to blow your whole stinking cruiser into its composite atoms and scatter them across the Galaxy like so much interstellar dust, *that's* why. Kirk out."

McCoy was looking at him, wide-eyed. "The Council sent you here on a diplomatic mission," he said, a grin lighting up his face. "That was not the most diplomatic speech I've ever heard."

"Maybe not, Bones," Kirk said, returning the grin, "but after all these hours of waiting, it sure felt good." He swiveled in his chair and began issuing orders. "Phaser crews, stand by in case of attack. Mr. Scott, prepare to lower our shields and beam Spock and Tremain aboard. If the entire operation takes more than thirty seconds, Scotty, I'll have you demoted."

"If it takes more than thirty seconds, Captain," said the Chief Engineer, "I'll deserve it!"

On board the Romulan ship, Maximinus Thrax and his son Licinius stared wide-eyed at the broadcast from the Federation vessel. It was quite clear to them that Captain Kirk had gone stark, raving mad. "He acts like he's won a victory while at the same time capitulating," Licinius said, awe in his voice. "What does he know about that planet that we don't? Are you going to let him beam his crewmembers up, Father?"

The Commander stood facing the viewscreen, shoulders back and face set in an expression of stern pride. He was all that a Romulan Commander should be "Yes," he said, "I will let Kirk beam his people up. But, if it is a trap, I will destroy him . . . or he will destroy me. But I will die a Romulan—and I shall take the risk of being wrong."

His body sagged slightly from the effort of being what he once was. "I will win. I must win!" He turned to Licinius almost as if seeking approval, and then changed his mind. Thrax turned his head and said, "You needn't say anything, my son, either for or against my opinion. I am the Commander here, and I will act the part even if we all must die for it. Contact the *Enterprise* and tell Kirk he may lower his shields to beam up his crewmembers—and then let us prepare to die with honor if this is another of Kirk's treacheries."

Kirk was both surprised and pleased to receive the acknowledgment from the Romulan cruiser. Uhura turned to give him the message. "They say we can go ahead and beam our party up," the Communications Officer told him, "and that they won't open fire while our shields are down."

"Isn't trust wonderful?" McCoy commented.

"If nothing else, Bones, we can always trust in the Law of the Jungle." James Kirk smiled—a confident, catlike smile. "I roared the loudest, and they turned belly up. They get that ridiculous planet, I get my people—and I win. Their concession assures that."

"But you made a concession too, Captain," Ensign Chekov said. "You conceded the entire planet, without specific instructions from Star Fleet. . . ."

"Star Fleet will back me up, I'm sure. What's two or three hours? It's going to be the Romulans' planet anyway." Kirk was almost euphoric; doing something positive after so many hours of inactivity was exhilarating. Right or wrong, he had acted—and that was what mattered. "All right, Mr. Scott, have your transporter crew commence beam-up. Then let's get the hell out of here."

Kirk waited until his engineer gave him the signal that the operation had worked successfully and Spock and Tremain were back on board. Then he turned to McCoy. "Bones, now it's your turn to earn your keep. Get down to the Transporter Room fast. And—keep him alive."

But Kirk found himself talking to empty space. The only reply was the hiss of the door to the turbolift. McCoy was already gone.

"Put the shields back up now, Mr. Sulu," Kirk ordered, "and prepare a course for the nearest starbase. Oh, and Uhura," he added, turning to the Communications Officer, "get me the Romulan ship again. I want to thank them."

When Commander Thrax's face appeared once more on the screen, Kirk smiled at him and said, "It's all yours now. I want you to enjoy it. But understand that should the Neutral Zone shift again and this system come back into Federation territory, we're going to remind you of how easily we let you have it this time. And we'll fully expect you to *let* us have it back again."

The expression on Thrax's face was one of amazement. "You mean we've won?" he squeaked. "It wasn't a trap? It wasn't some devious plot of yours, Kirk? You're really giving us the system? I don't believe it!"

Kirk nodded, smiling. He was enjoying every second of the Romulan's discomfiture. "It's all yours. And, by the way—watch out for the Arachnians."

Kirk didn't intend to tell them any more than that. He wanted to let the Romulans worry a little. If they were going to make contact with the Arachnians, let it be by their own methods. He smiled again at the Romulan and, in a gleeful gesture, waggled his fingers at him in farewell. Then he signaled Uhura, and the communication was broken.

20

Down in the Sick Bay, Katalya Tremain stood beside the Vulcan's bed. Spock had been unconscious for three days while his body mended. It had been an uphill battle, but McCoy had poured nearly every antitoxin available into the Vulcan's system in a heroic effort to counter the effects of the Arachnian poison. Spock was now out of danger, and McCoy's boasts about his healing abilities pushed to the very limits of hubris. There was an almost festive air aboard the *Enterprise*, the feeling of a mission well accomplished. Star Fleet, quite belatedly, had indeed backed James Kirk in every action he had taken during the Arachnae crisis. The only small island untouched by this euphoria was Spock's bed—and Katalya Tremain.

She'd spent the days thinking a great deal, and remembering; and there had been times when she'd stood clutching the side of the bed and sobbing for hours. She had not allowed McCoy to comfort her, but had merely told him that this was something she had to work through on her own.

Now she felt like a deserted beach after a storm. There was driftwood, broken seashells, and the smell of dead seacreatures drifting across her mind. She knew she would have to rebuild; she would have to go back in her memory to the very time of Selik's death and to the emotions she had blocked, and take a different path—one that did not lead to hating all Vulcans. It would be a painful process, but she would do it.

She looked down at Spock, lying peacefully asleep, and knew that one possible path was that she might fall in love with *this* Vulcan. But it was something she knew she must not do. Transferring the emotions from one being to another would not heal her. Even so, the Selik in her mind had told her that she must give this man whatever he demanded. She must wait until he awoke to find out what that demand might be—and, if it *was* her love, what she might answer.

Almost as though responding to her thoughts, Spock stirred and opened his eyes. He saw her bending over him, and a tiny twitch of a smile flickered there for a fraction of a second. "I see that you are still here, Dr. Tremain, and that I am alive. Are you pleased, or disappointed?"

"That's the sort of unpleasant, ungrateful question I would expect of a Vulcan," she smiled, taking the sting out of the words. "Of course I'm glad you're alive! If you'd died down there, I'd probably be standing court-martial for your murder." She turned away, studying the life-support panel. "I am glad, really I am," she muttered, half under her breath.

"I know that. I knew it from the moment I met you, that it was all a false front—not very original, and not very logical. I do hope you can avoid it in the future."

"I did promise you on Arachnae that I would try. I intend to keep that promise. I probably will go to Vulcan itself and try to rid myself of the toxins in my mind by overdosing on Vulcans. And if that doesn't work—well, as I've said before, it's wise to know as much as possible about one's enemies."

"And after you are well, what then?" Spock asked. "Are you coming back to the *Enterprise?* Dr. McCoy wishes it, you must know—and not just for professional reasons, either. I am afraid he has developed some sort of emotional bond toward you. But that is your problem and, thankfully, not mine to deal with."

"It all depends on what you expect of me. Getting over hating Vulcans was a promise I made to you when I thought you were dying. But I'm not sure if that's what our bargain really was. You didn't ask anything for yourself, Spock."

Spock nodded quietly, reaching his arms up and interlaced his fingers behind his head. He stretched, enjoying the feeling. "Then you feel you still owe me something? I do hope you're not going to offer yourself to me, or something equally silly. The idea of your transferring your feelings for Selik to me is extremely distasteful. Having Christine Chapel love me is quite sufficient to disturb my Vulcan mind; two Terrans in that unfortunate condition would be more than I could readily tolerate."

Tremain sighed with relief. "I had considered that possibility, and rejected it. It wouldn't work out. And as for Leonard, well, there is a chance of something happening between us, after I readjust my thinking. I have a lot of work to do before I could really love anyone. It may be Leonard, or then again, it might be Commodore Stone—who knows? I've got a lot of future ahead of me," she smiled down at the Vulcan, "and I owe that to you. There is one thing, though, that I have learned from both you and Selik—" She paused, waiting for him to ask what it might be.

Spock obliged readily. "Are you going to tell me what that one thing is, or do you intend to keep me in suspense?" His tone of voice was light—almost, but not quite, bantering.

"Yes, it's this." She reached up to touch her ears. "My ears are oddly shaped—they're round."

Spock nodded, trying hard not to grin, but pleased with the results of his tinkering with her mind—he had succeeded in getting Tremain to understand *something* from a Vulcan point of view. He was about to congratulate himself again when the door to the Sick Bay opened and Dr. McCoy came in.

"I could see from my monitors that you were finally awake," the doctor said. "And I thought I'd come in to see how you were before Katalya strangled you."

Spock and Tremain each raised an eyebrow in an almost identical Vulcan gesture. McCoy saw it and was vastly amused.

"I think there was very little danger of that, Doctor," Spock said. "And we have managed to solve the problem. Don't you agree, Dr. Tremain?"

"Oh, quite, Mr. Spock. I don't think there's any danger whatsoever of my killing you."

McCoy groaned as he comtemplated Tremain's quietly smiling face. "Don't tell me I've got another Christine Chapel on my hands. Please, Katalya, don't tell me that. If I lose you to this Vulcan, *I* may strangle him."

"No chance, Len. I'm not in love with Spock, and I never will be in love with Spock, so relax. Of course . . . I'm not in love with you either—yet. We'll have to see about that. And you will have to give me time —a lot of time, I'm afraid. That's the only promise I can give you now. Is it enough for you to wait and see what happens?"

McCoy nodded. He, too, was smiling. He reached out to hug Katalya, but stopped in midgesture when Spock cleared his throat noisily.

"If you two could possibly save your emotional exhibitionism until such time as you are out of my presence, I would appreciate it. I am still somewhat fatigued by my experiences, and I do not wish an additional overload of having to watch such a distasteful procedure. So if you don't mind, I would like you to leave."

Tremain nodded, starting to reach for McCoy's hand to lead him out of the room. "Oh, but there is one thing, Dr. Tremain," Spock added. "The debt you owe me. I know what it is. When you are finished detoxifying yourself on Vulcan and you return to the *Enterprise*—as I am sure you will—there is something

I want you to do for me." The Vulcan paused, searching for the right words with which to express himself. "I want you to give me what I never had as a child, that which I was not allowed to have as a child. Katalya," he said, looking directly at her, "I want you to give me an imagination. I want you to give me the possibility to consider all the alternatives—no matter how risky or how whimsical they might be. I want that from you, Katalya. In fact, I demand it from you."

"It's a very small price to pay, Spock. And one that I'm very honored that you would ask of me." She smiled at him, a warm smile devoid of any hatred or dislike. "I will do everything in my power to give that to you. And not just because you ask it, but because—" She tilted her head a little to one side. "—because I like you, Mr. Spock, and because I admire you. Now, Len, shall we go off and do our disgusting emotional exhibition elsewhere?"

McCoy took her hand and then turned to face the Vulcan. "Do you know, Spock, I am almost considering having you up on charges for practicing psychiatry without a license—but the results are so marvelous that I think I may ask for a medal for you instead."

Spock smiled and refrained from comment.

THE EXCITING REALM OF STAR TREK

☐	2151	STAR TREK LIVES!	$1.95
		by Lichtenberg, Marshak & Winston	
☐	2719	STAR TREK: THE NEW VOYAGES	$1.75
		by Culbreath & Marshak	
☐	11392	STAR TREK: THE NEW VOYAGES 2	$1.95
		by Culbreath & Marshak	
☐	10159	SPOCK, MESSIAH! A Star Trek Novel	$1.75
		by Cogswell & Spano	
☐	10978	THE PRICE OF THE PHOENIX	$1.75
		by Marshak & Culbreath	
☐	11145	PLANET OF JUDGMENT	$1.75
		by Joe Haldeman	
☐	11802	MUDD'S ANGELS	$1.75
		by J. Lawrence	

THRILLING ADVENTURES IN INTERGALACTIC SPACE
BY JAMES BLISH

☐	10797	SPOCK MUST DIE!	$1.50
☐	10835	STAR TREK 1	$1.50
☐	10811	STAR TREK 2	$1.50
☐	10818	STAR TREK 3	$1.50
☐	10812	STAR TREK 4	$1.50
☐	10840	STAR TREK 5	$1.50
☐	11697	STAR TREK 6	$1.50
☐	10815	STAR TREK 7	$1.50
☐	10816	STAR TREK 8	$1.50
☐	12111	STAR TREK 9	$1.75
☐	11992	STAR TREK 10	$1.75
☐	11417	STAR TREK 11	$1.50
☐	11382	STAR TREK 12	$1.75

Buy them at your local bookstore or use this handy coupon for ordering:

Bantam Books, Inc., Dept. ST, 414 East Golf Road, Des Plaines, Ill. 60016

Please send me the books I have checked above. I am enclosing $_____
(please add 50¢ to cover postage and handling). Send check or money order
—no cash or C.O.D.'s please.

Mr/Mrs/Miss_____

Address_____

City_____State/Zip_____

ST—8/78

Please allow four weeks for delivery. This offer expires 11/78.

Bantam Book Catalog

Here's your up-to-the-minute listing of over 1,400 titles by your favorite authors.

This illustrated, large format catalog gives a description of each title. For your convenience, it is divided into categories in fiction and non-fiction—gothics, science fiction, westerns, mysteries, cookbooks, mysticism and occult, biographies, history, family living, health, psychology, art.

So don't delay—take advantage of this special opportunity to increase your reading pleasure.

Just send us your name and address and 50¢ (to help defray postage and handling costs).